Fawcett Books
by Alistair MacLean:

BEAR ISLAND

THE BLACK SHRIKE

BREAKHEART PASS

CARAVAN TO VACCARES

CIRCUS

FEAR IS THE KEY

FORCE 10 FROM NAVARONE

THE GOLDEN GATE

THE GOLDEN RENDEZVOUS

GOODBYE CALIFORNIA

THE GUNS OF NAVARONE

H.M.S. ULYSSES

ICE STATION ZEBRA

NIGHT WITHOUT END

PUPPET ON A CHAIN

RIVER OF DEATH

THE SATAN BUG

SEAWITCH

THE SECRET WAYS

THE WAY TO DUSTY DEATH

WHEN EIGHT BELLS TOLL

WHERE EAGLES DARE

RIVER OF DEATH

ALISTAIR MacLean

FAWCETT CREST • NEW YORK

Library of Congress Catalog Card Number: 81-43305

ISBN 0-449-20058-2

Printed in the United States of America

First International Edition: March 1982

First Fawcett Crest Edition: April 1983

10 9 8 7 6 5 4 3 2 1

RIVER
OF DEATH

DARKNESS WAS FALLING OVER the ancient Grecian monastery and the first of the evening stars were beginning to twinkle in the cloudless Aegean sky. The sea was calm, the air was still, and it did, as is so often claimed, smell of wine and roses. A yellow moon, almost full, had just cleared the horizon and gave its soft and benign light to the softly rolling landscape, lending a magical quality to the otherwise harsh, forbidding outlines of the black and brooding monastery which, any evidence to the contrary, slumbered on peacefully as it had done for countless centuries gone by.

At that moment, unfortunately, conditions inside the monastery could hardly be said to reflect the dreamlike outer world. Magic had taken wings, no one slumbered, the peace was broken, darkness had given way to a score of smoking oil torches, and there was little around in the way of wine and roses.

Eight uniformed members of the Nazi S.S. were carrying oaken chests across the flagged hallway. The brass-bound boxes were small but so heavy that it required four men to carry one of them: A sergeant supervised their operations.

Watching them were four men. Two of those were high-ranking S.S. officers: of those, one, Wolfgang Von Manteuffel, a tall, thin man with cold blue eyes, was a major-general, no more than thirty-five years old; the second, Heinrich Spaatz, a thickset, swarthy man who had apparently elected a scowl as his permanent expression in life, was a colonel of thirty-seven. The other two watchers were monks in cowled brown habits, old proud men but now with mingled fear and pride in their eyes, eyes that never left the oaken chests. Von Manteuffel touched the sergeant with the tip of his gold-handled malacca cane which could hardly have been regulation issue to S.S. officers.

"A spot check, I think, Sergeant."

The sergeant gave orders to the nearest group who, not without difficulty, lowered their chest to the floor. The sergeant knelt, knocked away the retaining pins in the iron hasps, and lifted the hinged lid, the screeching of the ancient metal testimony enough to the fact that many, many years must have passed since this had last been done. Even in the wavering light of the malodorous oil torches the revealed contents glittered as if alive. The chest contained literally thousands of golden coins, so fresh and gleaming they could have been minted that same day. Von Manteuffel contemplatively

tirred the coins with the tip of his cane, looked
with satisfaction at the resulting iridescence, then
urned to Spaatz.

"Genuine, you would say, Heinrich?"

"I am shocked," Spaatz said. He didn't look it.
"Shocked beyond words. The holy fathers traffic in
dross?"

Von Manteuffel shook his head sadly. "You can't
rust anyone these days."

With what appeared to be as much a physical
effort as an exercise of will, one of the monks
averted his fascinated gaze from the glittering chest
to look at Von Manteuffel. He was a very slender
man, very stooped, very old—nearer ninety than
eighty. His face was carefully expressionless, but
there wasn't much he could do about his stricken
eyes.

"These treasures are God's," he said, "and we
have guarded them for generations. Now we have
broken our trust."

"You can't take all the credit for that," Von
Manteuffel said. "We helped. Don't worry, we'll look
after them for you."

"Yes, indeed," Spaatz said. "Be of good cheer,
Father. We shall prove worthy of our stewardship."

They stood in silence until the last of the treasure
chests was removed, then Von Manteuffel gestured
toward a heavy oaken door.

"Join your comrades. I'm sure you will be released as soon as our planes are heard to leave."

The two old men, clearly as broken in spirit as
they were in body, did as ordered, Von Manteuffel

closing the door behind them and sliding home the
two heavy bolts. Two troopers entered, carrying a
fifty-liter drum of petrol which they laid on its side
close to and facing the oaken door. It was clear that
they had been well briefed in advance. One trooper
unscrewed the cap of the petrol drum while the
other laid a trail of gunpowder to the outside doorway. More than half of the petrol gushed out onto
the flags, some of it seeping under the oaken door.
The trooper seemed content that the rest of the
petrol should remain inside the drum.

Following the departing troopers, Von Manteuffel and Spaatz walked away and halted at the
outside doorway. Von Manteuffel struck a match
and dropped it on the gunpowder fuse: For all the
expression that his face registered, he could have
been sitting in a church.

The airfield was only a two minutes' walk, and
by the time the S.S. officers arrived there the troopers had finished loading and securing the chests
aboard the two Junkers 88's, engines already running, parked side by side on the tarmac. At a word
from Von Manteuffel, the troopers ran forward and
scrambled aboard the second plane: Van Manteuffel and Spaatz, doubtless to emphasize the superiority of the officer class, sauntered leisurely to
the first. Three minutes later both planes were airborne. In robbery, looting, and plundering, as in all
else, Teutonic efficiency shone through.

At the rear of the lead plane, beyond rows of
boxes secured to painstakingly prepared racks on
the floor, Von Manteuffel and Spaatz sat with glasses

in their hands. They appeared calm and unworried and had about them the air of men secure in the knowledge that behind lay a job well done. Spaatz glanced casually out of a window. He had no trouble at all in locating what he knew he was bound to see.

A thousand, maybe fifteen hundred feet below the gently banking wing, a large building burned ferociously, illuminating the landscape, shore, and sea for almost half a mile around. Spaatz touched Von Manteuffel on the arm and pointed. Von Manteuffel glanced through the window and almost immediately looked indifferently away.

"War is hell," he said.

He sipped his cognac, looted, of course, from France, and touched the nearest chest with his cane. "Nothing but the best for our fat friend. What value would you put on our latest contribution to his coffers?"

"I'm no expert, Wolfgang." Spaatz considered. "A hundred million deutsche marks?"

"A conservative estimate, my dear Heinrich. Very conservative. And to think he already has a thousand million overseas."

"I've heard it was more. In any event, we will not dispute the fact that the fieldmarshal is a man of gargantuan appetites. You only have to look at him. Do you think *he* will some day look at *this*?" Von Manteuffel smiled and took another sip of his cognac. "How long will it take to fix things, Wolfgang?"

"How long will the Third Reich last? Weeks?"

"Not if our beloved Fuehrer remains as commander-in-chief."

Spaatz, thickset, looked gloomy and slid down in his seat. "And I, alas, am about to join him in Berlin where I shall remain to the bitter end."

"The *very* end, Heinrich?"

Spaatz grimaced. "A hasty amendment. Almost the bitter end."

"And I shall be in Wilhelmshaven."

"Naturally. A code word?"

Von Manteuffel pondered briefly, then said, " 'We fight to the death.' "

Spaatz sipped his cognac and smiled sadly. "Cynicism, Wolfgang, never did become you."

AT THE BEST OF TIMES THE DOCKS at Wilhelmshaven would have no difficulty in turning away the tourist trade. And that present moment was not the best of times. It was cold and raining and very dark. The darkness was quite understandable for the port was bracing itself for the now inevitable attack by the R.A.F.'s Lancasters on the North Sea submarine base, or what, by this time, was left of it. Yet there was one small area of illumination and subdued illumination, coming from low-powered lamps in hooded shades. Faint though this area of light was, it still contrasted sufficiently with the blackness around to offer marauding bombers a pinpoint identification marker for bombardiers crouched in the noses of the planes of the surely approaching squadrons. No one in Wilhelmshaven was happy about those lights, but then no one was anxious to question the orders of the S.S.

general responsible for their being switched on, especially when that general was carrying with him the personal seal of Fieldmarshal Goering.

General Von Manteuffel stood on the bridge of one of the latest of the German Navy's long-range U-boats. Beside him stood an apprehensive U-boat captain who didn't relish the prospect of being caught moored alongside a quay when the R.A.F. appeared. He had about him the air of a man who would have loved nothing better than to pace up and down in an agony of frustration, only there isn't much room for pacing on the conning tower of a submarine. He cleared his throat in the loud and unmistakable fashion of one who is not about to speak lightly and looked up at the taller officer.

"General Von Manteuffel, I must insist that we leave now. Immediately. We are in mortal danger."

"My dear Captain Reinhardt, I don't fancy mortal danger any more than you do." Von Manteuffel didn't give the impression of caring about any danger, mortal or otherwise. "But the Reichmarshal has a very short way of dealing with subordinates who disobey his orders."

"I'll take a chance on that." Captain Reinhardt didn't just sound desperate, he was desperate. "I'm sure Admiral Doenitz—"

"I wasn't thinking about you and Admiral Doenitz. I was thinking about the Reichmarshal and myself."

"Those Lancasters carry ten-ton bombs," Reinhardt said unhappily. "Ten tons! It took only two to finish off the *Tirpitz*. The *Tirpitz*, the most powerful battleship in the world. Can you imagine—"

"I can imagine all too well. I can also imagine the wrath of the Reichmarshal. It exceeds ten tons. The second truck, God knows why, has been delayed. We stay."

He turned and looked along the quay where groups of men were hurriedly unloading boxes from a military truck and staggering with them across the quay and up the gangway to an opened hatchway for'ard of the bridge. Small boxes but inordinately heavy. No one had to exhort those men to greater effort: They, too, knew all about the Lancasters and were as conscious as any of the imminent threat to their lives.

A bell rang on the bridge. Captain Reinhardt lifted a phone, listened, then turned to Von Manteuffel.

"A top priority call from Berlin, General. You can take it from here or privately below."

"Here will do," Von Manteuffel said. He took the phone from Reinhardt. "Ah! Colonel Spaatz."

"We fight to the death," Spaatz said. "The Russians are at the gates of Berlin."

"My God! So soon?" Von Manteuffel appeared to be genuinely upset at the news as, indeed in the circumstances, he had every right to be. "My blessings on you, Colonel Spaatz. I know you will do your duty by the Fatherland."

"As will every true German." Spaatz's tone, overheard by Captain Reinhardt, was a splendid amalgam of resolution and resignation. "We fall where we stand. The last plane out leaves in five minutes."

"My hopes and prayers are with you, my dear Heinrich. Heil Hitler!"

Von Manteuffel handed back the phone, looked out toward the quay, stiffened, then turned urgently toward the captain.

"Look there! The second truck has just arrived. Every man you can spare for the job!"

"Every man I can spare for the job is already on the job." Captain Reinhardt seemed oddly resigned. "They all want to live just as much as you and I do."

HIGH ABOVE THE NORTH SEA THE air thundered and reverberated to the throbbing roar of scores of plane engines. On the Lancaster flight deck of the point plane of the squadrons, the captain turned to his navigator.

"Our E.T.A. over target area?"

"Twenty-two minutes," the navigator said. "Heaven help those poor sods in Wilhelmshaven tonight."

"Never mind about the poor sods in Wilhelmshaven," the captain said. "Spare a thought for us poor sods up here. We must be on their screens by now."

At that moment another aircraft, a Junkers 88, was approaching Wilhelmshaven from the east. There were only two people aboard, which seemed a poor turnout for what was supposed to be the last plane out of Berlin. Colonel Spaatz, seated beside the pilot, looked uncommonly nervous and unhappy, a state of mind that was not induced by the fact that their Junkers was being almost continuously bracketed by exploding antiaircraft shells— or the knowledge that practically the entire length of their flight lay over what was now Allied-occupied territory. Colonel Spaatz had other things on his mind. He glanced anxiously at his watch and turned impatiently to the pilot.

"Faster, man! Faster!"

"Impossible, Colonel."

Both troopers and seamen were working in a frenzy of activity to transfer the remaining treasure chests from the second military truck to the submarine. Suddenly, the air-raid warning sirens began their ululating banshee wailing. As if by command, and in spite of the fact that they had known this was inevitable, the workers stopped and looked up fearfully into the night sky. Then, once more, again as if by command, they resumed their frantic efforts. It would have appeared impossible that they could have improved their previous work rate, but they unquestionably did. It is one thing to be almost certain that the enemy may appear at any time: It is quite another to have the last lingering vestiges of hope vanish and know that the Lancasters are upon you.

Five minutes later the first bomb fell.

Fifteen minutes later the entire Wilhelmshaven naval base appeared to be on fire. Clearly, this was no run-of-the-mill raid. By this time Von Manteuffel could have ordered the most powerful arc lamps to be switched on and it wouldn't have made the slightest difference. The entire dock area was an inferno of dense and evil-smelling smoke shot through with great columns of flame, through which shadowy Dantesque figures moved as in some nameless nightmare, seemingly as oblivious of their surroundings as they were of the screaming plane engines, the ear-numbing explosion of bombs, the sharp whiplike cracks of heavy antiaircraft fire, the ceaseless stuttering of machine guns, although what the machine guns hoped to achieve was difficult to imagine. Through all this the S.S. men and seamen, reduced now, despite all their will, to almost zombie-like slow motion by the increasingly heavy burden of the chests, continued their fatalistic loading of the submarine.

On the conning tower, both Von Manteuffel and Captain Reinhardt were coughing harshly as the heavy, corrosive smoke from the burning oil tanks enveloped them. Tears streamed down the cheeks of both men.

Captain Reinhardt said, "God's sake, man, that last one was a ten-tonner. And straight on top of the U-boat pens. Concrete ten feet thick, twenty, what does it matter? There can't be one of our people left alive there now, the concussion will have killed them all. In heaven's name, General, let's *go*. We've had the devil's own luck till now. We can come back when it's all over."

"Look, my dear Captain, the air raid is at its

height now. Try moving out of the harbor now, a slow business as you know, and you have as good a chance of being blown out of the water as you have alongside the quay here."

"Maybe so, Herr General, maybe so. But at least we'd be *doing* something." Reinhardt paused, then went on, "If I may say so without offense, sir, surely you must know that a captain is in command of his own vessel."

"Even as a soldier I know that, Captain. I also know that you're not in command until you have cast off and are under way. We complete loading."

"I could be court-martialled for saying this. But you are inhuman, General. The devil rides your back."

Von Manteuffel nodded.

"He does, he does."

At THE WILHELMSHAVEN AIR-field a dimly seen plane, eventually identifiable as a Junkers 88, makes so violent a touchdown that its undercarriage could well have collapsed under the impact. The bumpiness was understandable, the drifting smoke being so intense that the pilot could make only a blind guess as to his height above the runway. Under normal conditions he would never have dreamed of attempting so hazardous a landing. But conditions were far from normal. This Colonel Spaatz was a man of a highly persuasive cast of mind. Even before the plane had rolled to rest he had the door open, peering anxiously for his waiting transport. When finally he saw it—an open Mercedes staff car—he was aboard it within twenty seconds, urging the driver to make all possible haste.

The smoke surrounding the submarine was, if anything, even denser and more acrid than it had

15

been minutes before, although a sudden gusting wind, no doubt the result of the firestorm, gave promise of an early amelioration of the conditions. But choking and half-blinding though the smoke still was, it didn't prevent Von Manteuffel from seeing what, despite his coolly relaxed calm, he had so desperately wanted to see.

"That's it, then, Captain Reinhardt, that's it. The last chest aboard. And now your men aboard, Captain, and let the devil ride on *your* back."

Captain Reinhardt was not in the frame of mind to require any second bidding. Shouting hoarsely to make himself heard above the still thunderous din, he ordered his men aboard, ropes to be cast off, and engines slow ahead. The last of his men were still frantically climbing up the sliding gangway as the submarine inched away from the quayside. It hadn't moved more than a few feet when the sound of a motor car screeching and skidding to a halt made Von Manteuffel turn sharply and look at the quay.

Spaatz had leaped from the Mercedes while it was still moving. He stumbled, recovered himself, and stared at the still slowly moving submarine, his face contorted in desperate anxiety.

"Wolfgang!" Spaatz's voice wasn't a shout, it was a scream. "Wolfgang! *God's sake,* wait!" Then the anxiety on his face yielded abruptly to an expression of utter incredulity: Von Manteuffel had a pistol lined up on him. For some seconds Spaatz remained quite still, shocked into frozen and uncomprehending immobility; then comprehension

came with the crack of Von Manteuffel's pistol and
he hurled himself to the ground as a bullet struck
only a foot away. Spaatz dragged his Luger from
its holster and emptied it after the slowly moving
submarine which, apart from giving vent to his feelings, was an otherwise futile gesture: The conning
tower was empty. Von Manteuffel and Captain
Reinhardt had ducked beneath the shelter of the
steel walls off which Spaatz's bullets ricochetted
harmlessly. And then, abruptly, the submarine was
lost in swirling banks of smoke.

Spaatz pushed himself to his hands and knees and
stood upright to stare in bitter fury in the direction
of the vanished submarine.

"May your soul rot in hell, Major-General Von
Manteuffel," Spaatz said softly. "The Nazi Party's
funds. The S.S. funds. Part of Hitler's and Goering's
private fortunes. And now our treasures from
Greece. My dear and trusted friend."

He smiled almost reminiscently.

"But it's a small world, Wolfie. A small world,
and I'll find you. Besides, the Third Reich is gone.
A man must have something to live for."

Unhurriedly, he reloaded his Luger, brushed the
mud and moisture from his clothes, and walked
steadily toward the Mercedes staff car.

The pilot was in his seat, poring over a chart
when Spaatz clambered aboard the Junkers 88 and
took his seat beside him. The pilot looked at him
in mild astonishment.

Spaatz said, "Your tanks?"

"Full. I—I didn't expect you, Colonel. I was

about to leave for Berlin, as soon as the smoke clears."

"Madrid. The smoke has cleared."

"Madrid?" This time the astonishment was more than mild. "My orders—"

"Here are your new orders," Spaatz said. He produced his Luger.

ONE

THE CABIN OF THE THIRTY-SEATER aircraft was scruffy, battered, unclean, and more than a little noisome, which pretty accurately reflected the general appearance of the passengers. Even with other engines, they would never have made it to the ranks of the jet set. Two might have been classified as exceptions, or at least as being different, although neither would have made the jet-set division either, lacking, as they did, the pseudo-aristocratic veneer of your true wealthy and idle layabout.

One, who called himself Edward Hiller—in this remote area of southern Brazil it was considered poor form to go by your own name—was around thirty-five, stocky, fair-haired, hard-faced, a European or an American, and dressed in tan bush drills. He seemed to spend most of his time moodily examining the scenery, which, in truth, was hardly worth the examination, inasmuch as it duplicated tens of thousands of square miles in that virtually unknown part of the world: All that was to be seen was an Amazonian tributary meandering its way through the endless green of the rain forest of the Planalto de Mato Grosso.

The second exception—again because he seemed not unacquainted with the principles of basic hygiene—claimed to be called Serrano. He was dressed in an off-white suit, was about the same age as Hiller, slender, black haired, black moustached, swarthy. He could have been Mexican. He wasn't examining the scenery: He was examining Mr. Hiller, closely.

"We are about to land at Romono."

The loudspeaker was scratchy, tinny, the words almost indistinguishable.

"Please fasten seat belts."

The plane banked, lost altitude rapidly, and made its approach directly above and along the line of the river. Several hundred feet below the flight path a small, open outboard motorboat was making its slow way upstream.

This craft—on closer inspection a very dilapidated craft—had three occupants. The largest, John Hamilton, was tall, broad-shouldered, powerfully built, and forty years of age. He had keen brown eyes. The eyes were about the only identifiable feature of his face as he was uncommonly dirty, disheveled, and unshaven, giving the impression that he had recently endured some harrowing ordeal, an impression heightened by the fact that his filthy clothes were torn and his face, neck, and shoulders were liberally bloodstained. Comparatively, his two companions were presentable. They were lean, wiry, and at least ten years younger than Hamilton. Their olive-tinged faces were lively, humorous, and intelligent and they looked so much alike that they could have been identical twins, which they were. For reasons best known to themselves they liked to be known as Ramon and Navarro. They considered Hamilton—whose given name was, oddly enough, Hamilton—with critical and speculative eyes.

Ramon said, "You look bad."

Navarro nodded his agreement. "Anyone can see he's been through a lot. You think he looks bad enough?"

"Maybe not," Ramon said judicially. "A soupçon, perhaps. A little touch here, a little touch there." He leaned forward and proceeded to widen some of the already existing rents in Hamilton's clothing. Navarro stooped, touched a small animal lying on the floorboards, brought up a bloodied hand and added a few more artistically decorative crimson touches to Hamilton's face, neck and chest, then leaned back to examine his handiwork critically. He appeared more than satisfied with the result of his creative handiwork.

"My God!" He shook his head in sorrowful admiration. "You really have had it rough, Mr. Hamilton."

* * *

The faded, peeling sign on the airport building—
hardly more than a shack—read: WELCOME TO
ROMONO INTERNATIONAL AIRPORT which was, in its
own way, a tribute to the blind optimism of the person who had authorized it or the courage of the man
who had painted it. No "international" plane had
ever landed or ever would land there, not only because no one in his right senses would voluntarily
come from abroad to visit Romono in the first place
but primarily because the single grass runway was
so short that no aircraft designed later than the
forty-year-old DC-3 could possibly land there.

The aircraft that had been making the downriver
approach landed and managed, not without some
difficulty, to stop just short of the ramshackle terminal. The passengers disembarked and made for the
waiting airport bus that was to take them into town.

Serrano kept a prudent ten passengers behind
Hiller but was less fortunate when they boarded the
bus. He found himself four seats ahead of Hiller
and therefore was in no position to observe him
anymore.

Instead, Hiller was now observing Serrano,
thoughtfully.

Hamilton's boat was closing in on the riverbank.
"However humble," he said, "there's no place like
home."

Using "humble," Hamilton was guilty of grave
understatement. Romono was not just a jungle slum,

it was an outstandingly malodorous example of the
genre. On the left bank of the aptly named Rio da
Morte, it stood partly on a filled-in, miasmic swamp,
partly in a clearing that had been painfully hacked
out from a forest that pressed in menacingly on every
side, anxious to reclaim its own. The town looked
as if it might contain perhaps three thousand in-
habitants: Probably there were double that number
as three or four persons to a room was the accommodation norm of Romono. A typically end-of-the-
line—only there was no line—frontier town, it was
squalid, decaying, and singularly unprepossessing,
a maze of narrow, haphazardly crisscrossing alleys
—by no stretch of the imagination could they have
been called streets—with buildings ranging from
dilapidated wooden shacks through wine shops,
gambling dens, and bordellos to a large and largely
false-fronted hotel rejoicing, according to a garish
blue neon sign, in the name of the OTEL DE ARIS,
some misfortune having overtaken the missing
capitals H and P.

The waterfront was splendidly in keeping with
the town. It was difficult to say where the river ended
and the riverbank began for almost all of it was
lined with houseboats—there had to be some name
for those floating mistakes—relying for their con-
struction almost entirely on tar paper. Between the
houseboats were piles of driftwood, oil cans, bottles,
garbage, sewage, and swarms of flies. The stench
was overwhelming. Hygiene, had it ever come to

Romono, had abandoned it a long time ago as a lost cause.

The three men reached the bank, disembarked, and tied up the boat. Hamilton said, "When you're ready, take off for Brasilia. I'll join you in the Imperial."

Navarro said, "Draw your marble bath, my Lord? Lay out your best tuxedo?"

"Something like that. Three suites, the best. After all, we're not paying for it."

"Who is?"

"Mr. Smith. He doesn't know it yet, of course, but he'll pay."

Ramon said curiously, "You know this Mr. Smith? Met him, I mean?"

"No."

"Then might it be wise to wait for the invitation first?"

"No reason to wait. Invitation's guaranteed. Our friend must be nearly out of his mind by now."

"You're being downright cruel to that poor Mr. Hiller," Navarro said reproachfully. "He must have gone out of his mind during the three days we stayed with your Muscia Indian friends."

"Not him. He's sure he *knows* he knows." They started off. Hamilton called after them. "When you get to the Imperial keep close to a phone and away from your usual dives."

Ramon looked hurt. "There *are* no dives in our capital, Mr. Hamilton."

"You'll soon cure that."

Hamilton left them and made his way in the gathering dusk through winding, ill-lit alleyways until he had passed through the town and emerged on its western perimeter. Here, on the outskirts of the town and on the edge of the jungle, stood what had once passed for a log cabin but was now no more than a hut, and even at that, one would have thought, a hut scarcely fit for animal far less human habitation: The grass- and weed-covered walls leaned in at surreal angles, the door was badly warped, and the single window had hardly an unbroken pane of glass left in it. Hamilton, not without difficulty, managed to wrench open the creaking door and passed inside.

He located and lit a guttering oil lamp which gave off light and smoke in equal proportions. From what little could be seen from the fitful yellow illumination, the interior of the hut was a faithful complement of the exterior. The hut was sparsely furnished with the bare essentials for existence—a dilapidated bed, a couple of old bentwood chairs in no better condition than the bed, a warped deal table with two of the original three drawers, some shelving, and a cooker with traces of the original black enamel showing under the almost total covering of brown rust. On the face of it, John Hamilton didn't put much emphasis on the Sybaritic life.

He sat wearily on the bed which sagged and creaked in an alarmingly disconcerting fashion. Reaching under the bed, he came up with a bottle of indeterminate liquid, drank deeply from the neck, and set the bottle down unsteadily on the table.

Hamilton was observed. A figure had appeared just outside the window and was peering inside from a prudent distance, a probably unnecessary precaution. It is more difficult to see from a lighted area to a darkened one than the other way round, and the window was so covered with cobwebs that it was difficult to see through it anyway. The watcher's face was indistinct, but the identity of the man, had Hamilton been able to see him, would not have been hard to guess: He was probably the only man in Romono who wore a suit, far less an off-white one. His smile was composed of an odd mixture of amusement, satisfaction, and contempt.

Hamilton extracted two leather pouches from the torn remains of his buttoned pockets and poured the contents of one of them into the palm of his hand, staring in rapt admiration at the handful of rough-cut diamonds which he let trickle slowly onto the table. With an unsteady hand he fortified himself with another drink, then opened the other pouch, and emptied the contents. They were coins, golden coins. All told, there must have been at least fifty of them.

Gold, it is said, has attracted men from the beginning of recorded time. It unquestionably attracted the man at the window. Seemingly oblivious of the possibility of discovery, Serrano had moved closer, so close, indeed, that a keen-eyed and observant person inside the hut might well have seen the pale blur

of his face. But Hamilton was being neither keen-
eyed nor observant: He just continued to stare in
fascination at the treasure before him. So did Serrano. The amusement and contempt had disappeared from his face, the unblinking eyes seemed
huge, and his tongue licked his lips.

Hamilton took a camera from his rucksack, removed a cassette of exposed film, and examined it
closely for a moment; in doing so, he dislodged two
diamonds which fell and rolled under the table,
apparently unnoticed. He put the cassette on a shelf
beside some other cassettes and cheap camera
equipment, then turned his attention to the coins
again. He picked one up and examined it carefully,
almost as if seeing it for the first time.

The coin did not appear to be of any South
American origin—the likeness of the engraved head
was of classical Greek or Latin origin. He looked
at the obverse side: The characters, clear and un-
blemished, were unmistakably Greek.

Hamilton sighed, lowered some more of the rapidly diminishing contents of the bottle, returned the
coins to the pouch, paused as if in thought, shook
some coins into his hand, put them in a trouser
pocket, put the pouch into one of his buttoned shirt
pockets, returned the diamonds to their pouch and
his other buttoned pocket, had a last drink, turned
out the oil lamp, and left. He made no attempt to
lock the door for the sufficient reason that, even
with the door as fully closed as it would go, there
was still a two-inch gap between the key bolt and

doorjamb. Although it was by now almost dark he
did not appear to require any light to see where he
was going. Within a minute he had vanished into
the shantytown maze of corrugated iron, rotting
wood, and tar-paper shacks which formed the salu-
brious suburbs of Romono.

Serrano waited a prudent five minutes, then entered, a small flashlight in hand. He lit the oil lamp,
placing it on a shelf where it could not be seen directly from the outside; then, using his flashlight, he
located the fallen diamonds under the table and
placed them on the table. He crossed to the shelves,
took the cassette which Hamilton had placed there,
replaced it with another from the pile of cassettes,
and had just put the cassette on the table beside the
diamonds when he became suddenly and uncom-
fortably conscious of the fact that he was not alone.
He whirled around and found himself staring into
the muzzle of a rifle expertly and unwaveringly held
in Mr. Hiller's hand.

"Well, well," Hiller said genially. "A collector, I
see. Your name?"

"Serrano." Serrano didn't look any too happy.
"Why are you pointing that gun at me?"

"Calling cards you can't get in Romono, so I used
this instead. Are you carrying a gun, Serrano?"

"No."

"If you are and I find it, I'm going to kill you."
Hiller was still geniality itself. "Are you carrying a
gun, Serrano?"

Serrano reached slowly for an inside pocket. Hiller said, "The classic way, of course, my friend. Finger and thumb on the barrel, then gently on the table."

Serrano carefully, as directed, produced a small snub-nosed automatic and laid it on the table. Hiller advanced and pocketed it, along with the diamonds and the cassette.

"You've been following me all day," Hiller said. "For hours before we boarded that plane. And I saw you the previous day and the day before that. In fact, I've seen you quite a few times in the past few weeks. You really should get yourself another suit, Serrano. A shadower in a white suit is no shadow at all."

His tone changed in a fashion that Serrano didn't care much for. "*Why* are you following me, Serrano?"

"It's not you I'm after," Serrano said. "We're both interested in the same man."

Hiller lifted his gun a perceptible inch. If he'd lifted it only one millimeter, it would have carried sufficient significance for Serrano.

"I'm not sure," Hiller said, "that I like being followed around."

"Jesus!" Serrano's apprehension had become marked. "You'd kill a man for a thing like that?"

"What are vermin to me?" Hiller said carelessly. "But you can stop knocking your knees together. I've no intention of killing you—at least, not yet. No, I wouldn't kill a man just for following me around. But I wouldn't draw the line at shattering a kneecap so that you couldn't totter around after me or anyone else for months to come."

"I won't talk," Serrano said fervently. "I swear to God I won't."

"Aha! That's interesting. If you were going to talk, who would you talk to, Serrano?"

"Nobody. Nobody. Who would I talk to? That was just a manner of speaking."

"Was it now? But if you *were* to talk, what would you tell them?"

"What could I tell them? All I know—well, I don't know, but I'm pretty sure—is that Hamilton is into something big. Gold, diamonds, something like that—he's found a pile somewhere. I know that you're on his track, Mr. Hiller. That's why I am following you."

"You know my name. How come?"

"You're a pretty important man around these parts, Mr. Hiller." Serrano was trying to be ingratiating, but he wasn't very good at it. A sudden thought appeared to occur to him for he brightened and said, "Seeing we're both after the same man, Mr. Hiller, we could be partners."

"Partners!"

"I can help you, Mr. Hiller." Serrano was eagerness itself, but whether from the prospect of partnership or an understandable desire not to be crippled by Hiller was difficult to know, "I *can* help you. I swear I can."

"A terrified rat will swear to anything."

"I can *prove* what I say." Serrano seemed to have regained a measure of confidence. "I can take you to within five miles of the Lost City."

Hiller's reaction was one of astonishment, followed by suspicion.

"What do you know about it?" He paused and recovered. "Well, I suppose everybody's heard about the Lost City. Hamilton's always shooting off his mouth about it."

"Mebbe so. Mebbe so." Serrano, sensing the change in the atmosphere, was almost relaxed now. "But how many have followed him four times to within a few miles of it?" If Serrano had been at the gambling table, he'd have leaned back in his chair, his trump card played.

Hiller had become very interested, even to the extent of lowering then pocketing his own gun.

"You have a rough idea where it is?"

"Rough?" Immediate danger past, Serrano invested himself with an air very close to benign superiority. "Close is more like it. Very close."

"Then if you've come all that close, why don't you go looking for it yourself?"

"Look for it myself?" Serrano looked shocked. "Hiller, you must be out of your mind. You don't understand what you're talking about. You got *any* idea what the tribes in that area are like?"

"Pacified, according to the Indian Protection Service."

"Pacified?" Serrano gave a contemptuous laugh. "Pacified? They're pacified the way the alligators

are pacified. There isn't enough money in the country to make those desk-bound pansies leave those
lovely air-conditioned offices in Brasilia and go see
for themselves. They're scared. Worse. They're terrified, plain terrified. Even their field agents—and
there are some pretty tough studs among them—
are terrified, won't go near the area."

He stopped, thought for a moment. "Well, four
of them did go there once some years back, but
none of them ever returned. And you know what?"

"No. What?"

"If they're terrified, Mr. Hiller, I'm terrified too."

"That creates quite a problem." Not surprisingly,
Hiller had become thoughtful. "An approach problem. What's so special about those bloodthirsty people? There are many tribes that don't care all that
much for people from the outside, what you and I
would regard as other civilized people." Apparently
Hiller saw nothing incongruous in categorizing Serrano as "civilized."

"Special? I'll tell you what's special about them.
They're the most savage tribes in the Mato Grosso.
Correction. They're the most savage tribes in the
whole of South America. Not one of them have
moved out of the Stone Age so far. In fact, they
must be a damned sight worse than Stone Age people. If Stone Age people had been like them, they'd
have wiped each other out. When those tribes there
have nothing better to do, they just go around mas-
sacring each other—to keep their hand in, you

know?—and there would have been no human left on this planet today."

He waved his arm.

"There are three tribes up there, Hiller. First, there are the Chapates. God knows they're bad enough. All they do is use their blowpipes, pump a few curare-tip poison darts into you, and leave you there. Almost 'civilized,' as you might say. Now the Horenas are different. They use darts that only knock you unconscious; then you're dragged back to their village and tortured to death—this, I understand, takes a day or two—then they cut off your head and shrink it. But when it comes to sheer butchery, you know, plain old savage stuff, the Muscias are the pick of the bunch."

"What's their specialty?"

"I don't think any white man has ever seen them. But one or two of the outside Indians who have met them and survived say that they're cannibals. They see what they think is an appetizing meal, they dump him alive into boiling water. Something like lobsters, you see. Go looking for a lost city surrounded by all those monsters? Why don't *you* go looking? I can point you in the right direction. Me, I only like cooking pots from the outside."

"Well, maybe I'll have to do a little more thinking on that one." Absently, almost, he handed Serrano back his gun. Hiller was no mean psychologist when it came to gauging the extent of a man's cupidity. Hiller said, "Where do you live?"

"A room in the Hotel de Paris."

"If you saw me in the bar there?"

"I've never seen you before in my life."

An unbiased guidebook to the taverns of South
America would have difficulty finding the space to
adequately describe the bar of the Hotel de Paris,
Romono, in its pages. The barroom was not a thing
of beauty. The indeterminately colored paint, what
little there was of it, was peeling and blistered, the
splintered wooden floor was blackened and filthy,
and the rough-cut soft-wood bar bore the imprints of
the passage of time. A thousand spilled drinks, five
thousand stubbed-out cigars and cigarettes. It was
not a place for the fastidious.

The clientele, fortunately, were not given to the
fastidious. Exclusively male and dressed for the
most part in scarecrow's clothing, they were coarse,
uncouth, ill-favored, and hard drinking. Especially
hard drinking. In season and at the right hour,
which is to say any month and any time of day, as
many customers as possible—and there were many
—pushed up to the bar and consumed quantities of
what could only be described as rotgut. The whiskey matched the decor. There were a scattering of
bentwood chairs and rickety tables, largely un-
occupied. For the first few hours, the citizens of
Romono were mostly vertical drinkers. Among the
currently vertical were both Hiller and Serrano,
separated from each other by a prudent distance.

In such surroundings, the entrance of John Hamilton did not provoke the horror-stricken reaction

that it would have in the plusher caravansaries of
Brasilia or Rio. Even so, his appearance was sufficiently interesting to cause a momentary marked
drop in the conversational level. With his tangled
hair, a week's growth of matted and bloodied beard,
and ripped and bloodstained shirt he looked as if
he had just returned from the scene of a successfully if messily executed triple murder. His expression—as was customary with him—lacked anything
in the way of encouragement toward chitchat. He
ignored the bleary, bloodshot stares, and although
the crowd before the bar was at least four deep, a
path opened before him, like a red-eyed sea. In
Romono, paths always opened for Hamilton, a man
obviously held, and for a variety of good reasons,
in considerable respect.

A large, fat barman, the boss of the four men
serving nonstop behind the bar, hurried forward.
His egg-bald pate gleamed in the light: Inevitably,
given the local gift for language, he was known as
Curly.

"Mr. Hamilton!"

"Whiskey."

"God's name, Mr. Hamilton. What happened?"

"You deaf?"

"Right away, Mr. Hamilton."

Curly reached under the bar, produced a special
bottle, and poured a generous measure. That Hamilton should be thus privileged apparently aroused no
resentment among the onlookers, not so much because of their innate courtesy, of which they had

none, but because Hamilton had demonstrated in the past his reaction to those who interfered in what he regarded as his own business: He'd only had to do it once, but once had been enough.

Curly's plump, genial face was alive with curiosity as were those of the bystanders. But, as everyone was well aware, Hamilton was not a man to share confidences. He tossed two Greek coins onto the bar. Hiller, who was standing close by, observed this and his face grew very still. His face was not the only one to assume sudden immobility.

"Bank's shut," Hamilton said. "Those do?"

Curly picked up the two shining coins and examined them with an air of unfeigned reverence.

"Will those do? *Will those do!* Yes, Mr. Hamilton, I think those will do. Gold. Pure gold! This is going to buy you an awful lot of scotch, Mr. Hamilton, an awful lot. One of those I'm going to keep for myself. Yes, sir. The other I'll take and have valued in the bank tomorrow."

"Up to you," Hamilton said indifferently.

Curly examined the coins more closely and said, "Greek, aren't they?"

"Looks like," Hamilton said with the same indifference. He drank some of his scotch and looked at Curly with a speculative eye. "You wouldn't, of course, be thinking of asking me if I went to Greece to get those?"

"Certainly not," Curly said hastily. "Certainly not. Will I—will I get the doctor, Mr. Hamilton?"

"Thanks. But it's not my blood."

"How many of them? Who did this to you—I mean, who did you do it to?"

"Just two. Horenas. Same again."

Although most people at the bar were still looking at Hamilton or the coins, the hubbub of conversation was slowly resuming. Hiller, glass in hand, elbowed his purposeful way toward Hamilton who saw him coming. He regarded Hiller's approach with his customary lack of enthusiasm.

Hiller said, "I hope you'll excuse me. I don't want to intrude, Mr. Hamilton. I understand that after tangling with headhunters a man would like some peace and quiet. But what I'd like to say to you is important. Believe me. Could I have a word?"

"About what?" Hamilton's tone was less than encouraging. "And I don't like discussing business —I assume it is business—with a dozen pairs of ears hanging onto every word."

Hiller looked around. Their conversation was attracting attention. Hamilton paused a moment, as if in thought, then picked up his bottle, jerked his head, and led the way to the corner table most remote from the bar. Hamilton, as always, looked aggressive and forbidding and when he sat down his tone matched his expression.

"Out with it," he said.

Hiller took no offense. "Suits me. That's the way I like it—the only way to do business. I'll lay it on the line. It's my belief you've finally found this Lost City of yours. I know a man who'd pay you a six-figure fee to take him there. That straight enough for you?"

"If you throw away that rubbish you have there I'll give you some decent scotch." Hiller did as requested and Hamilton topped up both glasses. Hiller knew that Hamilton was less interested in dispensing hospitality than in having time to think. From the just perceptibly slurred note in Hamilton's voice, it could well have been that he could be taking slightly longer than normal to think quickly and clearly.

"Well, I'll say this," Hamilton said, "you don't beat around the bush. Who says I've found the Lost City?"

"Nobody. How could they? No one knows where you go when you leave Romono—except maybe those two young sidekicks of yours." Hiller smiled thinly. "They don't look like the type that would talk too much."

"Sidekicks?"

"Oh, come off it, Hamilton. The twins. Everybody in Romono knows them. But it would be my guess that *you* would be the only person to know the exact location. So, okay, I'm only going on a hunch—and a couple of brand-new golden coins that may be a thousand years old, two thousand . . . Just supposing."

"Supposing what?"

"Supposing you'd found it, of course."

"Cruzeiros?"

Hiller kept his face impassive, a remarkable feat

in view of the wave of elation that had just swept through him. When a man talks money it means that he is prepared to sell, sure to dicker first, and eventually to make a deal, and Hamilton had the means to bargain. Hamilton had his price, his *quid pro quo,* and that could mean only one thing—he did know where the Lost City was. Fish hooked, Hiller thought exultantly: Now all we have to do is gaff and land him. That might well take time, Hiller knew, but he had every confidence in himself: He fancied his prowess as a fisherman.

"U.S. dollars," Hiller said.

Hamilton thought this over for a few moments, then said, "Attractive proposition. Very attractive. But I don't accept propositions from strangers. I don't know you, Hiller, what you are, what you do, and how come you're empowered to make this proposition."

"A con man, possibly?"

"Possibly."

"Oh, come. We've had a drink a dozen times in the past months. Strangers? Hardly. We all know why you've been searching those damned forests for the past four months and other huge stretches of the Amazon and Paraná basins for the past four or five years. For the fabled Lost City of the Mato Grosso—if that is indeed where it is—for the golden people who lived there—who may still live there—and most of all for the man who found it. Huston. Dr. Hannibal Huston. The famous explorer who vanished into the forests all those many years ago and was never seen again."

"You talk in clichés," Hamilton said.

Hiller smiled. "What newspaperman doesn't?"

"Newspaperman?"

"Yes."

"Odd. I'd have put you down for something else."

Hiller laughed. "A con? A convict on the lam? Nothing so romantic, I'm afraid." He leaned forward, suddenly serious. "Listen. As I said, we all know why you're out here—no offense, Hamilton, but goodness knows you've told everyone often enough—although why I don't know—I'd have thought you'd have kept it secret from everybody."

"Three good enough reasons, my friend. In the first place, there has to be some reason to account for my presence here. Second, anybody will tell you that I know the Mato Grosso better than any white man, and no one would dream of following me where I go. Finally, the more people who know what I'm after, the greater the likelihood that some person, some time and in some place, will drop a hint or a clue that could be useful to me."

"I was under the impression that you didn't require hints or clues any longer."

"That's okay. Just you go ahead and form any impressions you like."

"Well, all right. So, ninety-nine percent of the people laugh at your wild notions, as they call them —though God knows there's not a man in Romono would dare say it to your face. But I belong to the one percent. I believe you. I further believe that your search is over, that the dream has come true. I'd like to share in a dream, I'd like to help a man, my employer, make his dream come true."

"I'm deeply moved," Hamilton said sardonically. "I'm sorry—well, no, I'm not really—but something gives here that I just can't figure. And besides, Hiller, you are an unknown quantity."

"Is McCormick-Mackenzie International?"

"Is it what?"

"Unknown?"

"Of course not. One of the biggest multinationals in the Americas. Probably the usual bunch of crooks using the usual battery of crooked international lawyers to bend the laws any which way that suits them."

Hiller took a deep breath, manfully restraining himself. "Because I'm in the position of asking a favor of you, Hamilton, I won't take exception to that. In point of fact, the record of McCormick-Mackenzie is impeccable. They have never been investigated, far less impeached on any count."

"Smart lawyers. Like I said."

"You can be glad that Joshua Smith is not here to hear you say that."

Hamilton was unimpressed. "He the owner?"

"Yes. And the chairman and managing director and chief executive officer."

"The industrialist? Fat cat, many millions. If we're talking about the same man?"

"We are."

"*And* the owner of the largest newspaper and magazine chain in the Americas. Well, well, well." He broke off and stared at Hiller. "So that's why you—"

"Exactly."

"So. He's your boss. And you're one of his newspapermen, and a pretty senior one at that, I would guess—I mean, he wouldn't send out a cub reporter on a story like this. Very well. Your connections, your credentials established. But I still don't see—"

"What don't you see?"

"This man. Joshua Smith. Multimillionaire? A billionaire? Anyway, rich as Croesus. What's left on earth for him that he doesn't already have? What more can a man like that want?" Hamilton took a long pull at his whiskey. "In short, what's in it for him?"

"You are a suspicious bastard, aren't you, Hamilton? Money? Of course not. Are you in it for the money? Of course not. A man like you could make money anywhere. No. Like you—and, if I may say, a little bit like myself—he's a man with a dream, a dream that's become an obsession. I don't know which fascinates him the more, the Huston case or the Lost City, although I don't suppose you can really separate the two. I mean, you can't have the one without the other." He paused and smiled, almost dreamily. "And what a story for his publishing empire."

"And that, I take it, is your part of the dream?"

"What else?"

Hamilton considered, using some more scotch to help. "Mustn't rush things, mustn't rush things. A man needs time to think about these things."

"Of course. How much time?"

"Two hours?"

"Sure. My place. The Negresco." Hiller looked around him and gave a mock shudder. "It's almost as good as it is here."

Hamilton drained his glass, rose, picked up his bottle, nodded, and left. No one could have accused him of being under the weather, but his gait did not appear to be as steady as it had been. Hiller looked around until he located Serrano, who had been looking straight at him. Hiller glanced after the departing Hamilton, looked back at Serrano, and nodded almost imperceptibly. Serrano disappeared.

=TWO=

ROMONO HAD NOT YET GOT around to, and at the current rate of progress was unlikely ever to get around to, street lighting, with the result that the streets and alleyways, except for the saloons and bordellos fronting on them, tended to be poorly lit. Hamilton, all traces of his unsteady gait gone, strode briskly along, unbothered by the fitful or nonexistent lighting. He rounded a corner, carried on a few yards, stopped suddenly, and turned into a narrow and almost totally dark alleyway. He didn't go far into the alley—not more than two feet. He poked his head cautiously out from his narrow niche and peered back along the way he had just come.

He saw no more than he had expected to see. Serrano had just come into view. Serrano, clearly, wasn't out for any leisurely evening stroll. He was walking so quickly that he was almost running.

Hamilton shrank back into the shadows. He no longer had to depend on his hearing. Serrano was wearing steel-tipped shoes which no doubt he found indispensable for the subtler intricacies of his work. On a still night Serrano could have been heard a hundred yards away.

Hamilton, no more than another shadow in his shadowy place of concealment, listened to the rapidly approaching footsteps. Serrano, running now, looked neither to right nor to left but peered anxiously ahead, looking for his suddenly and mysteriously vanished quarry. He was still attempting to see through the murky lane ahead when he passed the alleyway entrance. Hamilton, a shadow detaching itself from the deeper shadow behind, stepped out swiftly and in silence brought his locked hands down on the base of Serrano's neck. He caught the already unconscious man before he could strike the ground and dragged him into the black concealment. From Serrano's breast pocket he removed a well-filled wallet, extracted a gratifying wad of cruzeiro notes, pocketed them, dropped the empty wallet on top of Serrano's prone form, and continued on his way, this time without a backward glance. He had no doubt that Serrano had been on his own.

Back in his tumbledown hut, the guttering oil lamp lit, Hamilton sat on his cot. Why had he been shadowed? That Serrano had acted under Hiller's instructions he was certain. He did not think that Serrano had intended to waylay or attack him. Hiller was almost desperately anxious to have his services, and an injured Hamilton would be the last thing he would want on his hands. Nor could robbery have been a motive—although they may well have seen the bulges of the two pouches in his shirt pockets, and Hamilton had been aware that Serrano had been watching him through the hut window. Petty theft would not have interested Hiller; what he was after was the pot of gold at the foot of the rainbow. And only Hamilton knew where that rainbow ended.

That Hiller and his boss Smith had dreams, Hamilton did not for a moment doubt. What he did doubt, and profoundly, was Hiller's own version of those dreams.

Hiller had wanted to find out if he had been going to contact his two young assistants or other unknown parties. Perhaps he thought that Hamilton might lead him to a larger and more worthwhile cache of gold and diamonds. Perhaps he thought Hamilton had gone to make some mysterious phone call. Perhaps anything. On balance, Hamilton thought, it was probably just because Hiller was of a highly suspicious nature and just wanted to know what, if anything, Hamilton was up to. There could be no other explanation, and it seemed pointless to waste further time and thought on it.

Hamilton poured himself a small drink—the nondescript bottle did in fact contain an excellent Highland malt that his friend Curly had obtained for him—and topped it up with bottled mineral water: The ordinary Romono water supply was an excellent specific for those who wished to be laid low with dysentery, cholera, or any of a variety of other unpleasant tropical diseases.

Hamilton smiled to himself. When Serrano came to and reported his woes to his master, neither ñe nor Hiller would wonder about the identity of the assailant responsible for the sore and stiff neck from which Serrano would assuredly be suffering. If nothing else, it would teach them to be rather more circumspect and respectful in their future dealings with him. Hamilton had no doubt whatsoever that he would be meeting Serrano again—officially—in the near future and would thereafter be seeing quite a deal of him.

Hamilton took a sip of his drink, dropped to his knees, ran his hand over the floor beneath the table, found nothing, and smiled. He crossed to the shelving, picked up a solitary cassette, examined it carefully, and smiled in even wider satisfaction. He drained his glass, turned out the light, and headed back into town.

In his room in the Hotel Negresco—the proprietors of the famous hotel in Nice would have cringed at the thought that such a hovel should bear the same name—Hiller was making—or trying to make—a telephone call, his face bearing the unmistakable expression that characterized any person so foolhardy as to try to phone out of Romono. But at long last his lack of patience was rewarded and his face lit up.

"Aha!" he said. His voice, understandably, had a

note of triumph in it. "At last, at last! Mr. Smith, if you please."

The drawing room of Joshua Smith's villa—the Villa Haydn in Brasilia—demonstrated beyond question the vast gulf that lay between him and the merely rich. The furnishings, mainly Louis XIV and not the shadow of an imitation in sight; the draperies, from Belgium and Malta; the carpets, ancient Persian to the last one; and the pictures, ranging all the way from old Dutch masters to the Impressionists, all spoke not only of immense wealth but an immense hedonistic determination to use it to its maximum. But for all that opulence there was nonetheless displayed an exquisite good taste. Everything matched or blended in something close to perfection. Clearly, no modern interior decorator had been allowed within a mile of the place.

The owner matched up magnificently. He was a large, well-built, and dinner-suited man of late middle age who looked absolutely at home in one of the huge armchairs that he occupied close to a pine-log fire. Joshua Smith, still dark in both hair and moustache, the one brushed straight back, the other neatly trimmed, was a smooth and urbane man, but not too smooth, not too urbane, much given to smiling, and invariably kind and courteous to his inferiors which, in his case, meant just about everybody in sight. In the passage of time, the carefully and painstakingly acquired geniality and urbanity had become second nature to him, although some of the original ruthlessness remained to account for his untold millions. Only a specialist could have detected the extensive, discreet plastic surgery that had transformed Smith's face from what it once had been.

There was another man in his drawing room, and a young woman. Jack Tracy was a young-middle-aged blond fellow, with a pockmarked face and a general air of capable toughness. The toughness and capability were genuine—they had to be for any man to be the general manager of Smith's vast chain of newspapers and magazines.

Maria Haller, with her slightly dusky skin and brown eyes, could have been South American, Southern Mediterranean, or Middle Eastern. Her hair was raven-colored. Whatever her nationality, she was indisputably beautiful, her face inscrutable, with watchful penetrating eyes. She didn't look kind or sensitive, but was both. She looked intelligent and had to be: When not doubling—as rumor had it—as Smith's mistress, she was his private and confidential secretary and it was no rumor that she was remarkably skilled in her official capacity.

The phone rang. Maria answered, told the caller to hold, and brought the phone on its extension cord across to Smith's armchair. He took the phone and listened briefly.

"Ah, Hiller!" Smith, unusually for him, leaned forward in his armchair. There was anticipation in his voice and posture. "You have, I trust, some encouraging news for me. You have? Good, good, good. Proceed."

Smith listened in silence to what Hiller had to say, the expression on his face gradually changing from pleasure to that of the near beatific. It was a measure of the man's self-control that, although apparently in a near transport of excitement, he refrained from either exclamations, questions, or interruptions and heard Hiller through in silence to the end.

"Excellent!" Smith was positively jubilant. "Truly excellent. Frederik, you have just made me the happiest man in Brazil." Although Hiller claimed to be called Edward, his true given name was known to Smith. "Nor, I assure you, will you have cause to regret this day. My car will meet you and your friends at the airport at eleven A.M." He replaced the receiver.

"I said I could wait forever," he said softly. "Forever is today."

Moments passed while he gazed sightlessly into the flames. Tracy and Maria looked at each other without expression. Smith sighed, gradually bestirred himself, leaned back into his armchair, reached into his pocket, brought out a gold coin, and examined it intently.

"My talisman," he said.

He still didn't appear to be quite with them. "Thirty long years I've had it, and I've looked at it every day in those thirty years. Hiller has seen this very coin. He says the ones this man Hamilton has are identical in every way. Hiller is not a man to make mistakes, so this can mean only one thing. Hamilton has found the foot of the rainbow."

Tracy said, "And at the far end of the rainbow lies a pot of gold?"

Joshua Smith looked at him without really seeing him. "Who cares," he whispered, "about the gold?"

There was a long and, for Tracy and Maria, uncomfortable silence. Smith sighed again and replaced the coin in his pocket.

"Another thing," Smith said, in a normal voice, enthusiasm restored. "Hamilton appears to have stumbled across some sort of an El Dorado."

"It seems less and less likely that this Hamilton is the kind of man to stumble across anything," Maria said. "He's a hunter, a seeker—not a stumbler. He has sources of information denied other so-called civilized people, especially among the tribes not yet classified as pacified. He starts off with some sort of clue that points him in the right direction, then starts quartering the ground, narrowing the area of search until he finally pinpoints what he's after. The element of chance doesn't enter into that man's calculations."

"You might be right, my dear," Smith said. "In fact you're almost certainly right. Anyway, what matters is that Hiller says that Hamilton seems to have located a diamond hoard."

Maria said, "War loot?"

"Overseas investments, my dear, overseas investments. Never 'loot.' In this case, however, no. They are uncut—rough-cut, rather—Brazilian diamonds. And Hiller is an expert on diamonds—God knows he's stolen enough in his lifetime. Anyway, it appears that Hamilton has fallen for Hiller's story, hook, line, and sinker—in Hiller's rather uninspired phrase. Two birds with one stone: He's found both the European gold and some Brazilian diamonds. Looks as if this is going to be even easier than we thought."

Tracy looked vaguely troubled. "He hasn't the reputation for being an easy man."

"Among the tribes of the Mato Grosso, agreed," Smith said. He smiled as if anticipating some future pleasure. "But he's going to find himself in a different kind of jungle here."

"Maybe you overlook one thing," Maria said soberly. "Maybe you're overlooking the fact that you've got to go back into the jungle with him."

THREE

Hiller, in his room in the Hotel Negresco, was studying a coin which he held in his hand when he was disturbed by an erratic knock on the door. He pulled out a gun, held it behind his back, crossed to the door, and opened it.

Hiller put his gun away. Serrano, both hands clutching the back of his neck, swayed dizzily and staggered into the room.

"Brandy!" Serrano's voice was a strangled croak.

"What the hell's happened to you?"

"Brandy!"

"Brandy coming up," Hiller said, resigned. He gave a generous double to Serrano, who downed it in a single gulp. The injured man had just finished his third brandy and was pouring out his tale of woe when another sharp rat-tat-tat came on the door, this knocking far from erratic. Again Hiller

55

took his precautionary measures, and again they proved unnecessary. The Hamilton who stood in the doorway was scarcely recognizable as the Hamilton of two hours previously. Two hours in the Hotel de Paris' grandiloquently named Presidential suite—no President had ever or would ever stay there, but it had the only bath in the hotel not corroded with rust—had transformed him. He had bathed and was clean-shaven. He wore a fresh set of khaki drills, a fresh khaki shirt without a rent in sight, and even a pair of gleaming new shoes.

Hiller glanced at his watch. "Two hours precisely. You are punctual."

"The politeness of princes."

Hamilton entered the room and caught sight of Serrano, who was busy pouring himself another large brandy. By this time it was difficult to judge whether he was suffering the more from the effects of the blow or the brandy. Holding the glass in one rather unsteady hand and massaging the back of his neck with the other, he continued the restorative ritual without seeming to notice Hamilton.

Hamilton said, "Who's this character?"

"Serrano," Hiller said. "An old friend." It would have been impossible to guess from Hiller's casual offhandedness that he'd met Serrano for the first time only that evening. "Don't worry. He can be trusted."

"Delighted to hear it," Hamilton said. He couldn't remember the month or the year when he last trusted anybody. "Makes a welcome change in this day and age." He peered at Serrano with the air of a concerned and kindly healer. "Looks to me as if he's coming down with something."

"He's been down," Hiller said. "Mugged." He was observing Hamilton closely but could have spared himself the trouble.

"Mugged?" Hamilton looked mildly astonished. "He was walking the streets this time of night?"

"Yes."

"And alone?"

"Yes," Hiller said, and added in what he probably regarded as a rather pointed fashion, *"You* walk alone at night."

"I know Romono," Hamilton said. "Much more importantly, Romono knows me." He looked pityingly at Serrano. "I'll bet you weren't even walking in the middle of the road—and I'll bet you're that much lighter by the weight of your wallet."

Serrano nodded, scowled, said nothing, and got back to his self-medication.

"Life's a great teacher," Hamilton said absently. "But it beats me how a citizen of Romono could be so damned stupid. Okay, Hiller, when do we leave?"

Hiller had already turned toward a glass-fronted wall cupboard. "Scotch?" he said. "No firewater. Guaranteed."

He showed Hamilton a famous proprietary brand of scotch with the seal unbroken.

"Thanks."

Hiller's gesture had not been motivated by an undiluted spirit of hospitality. He had turned his back on Hamilton to conceal what he knew must have been a momentary flash of triumph in his face: Moreover, this was definitely a moment for celebration. Back in the bar of the Hotel de Paris he had been sure that he had his fish hooked: Now he had it gaffed and landed.

"Cheers," he said. "We leave at first light tomorrow."

"How do we go?"

"Bush plane to Cuiabá." He paused, then added apologetically. "Rickety old bus of cardboard and wire, but it's never come down yet. After that, Smith's private jet. That's something else again. It will be waiting for us at Cuiabá."

"How do you know?"

Hiller nodded toward the phone. "Carrier pigeon."

"Pretty sure of yourself, weren't you?"

"Not really. We like to arrange things in advance. I just go on probabilities." Hiller shrugged. "One call to fix things, then another call to cancel. Then from Cuiabá to Smith's private airfield in Brasilia." He nodded toward Serrano. "He's coming with us."

"Why?"

"Why not?" Hiller even managed to look puzzled. "My friend. Smith's employee. Good jungle man."

"Always wanted to meet one of those." Hamilton looked consideringly at Serrano. "One can only hope that he's a little bit more alert in the depths of the Mato Grosso than in the alleys of Romono."

Serrano had nothing to say to this, but he was, clearly, and for the first time in hours, thinking. Prudently, he refrained from voicing his thoughts.

Joshua Smith, it would seem, was both a considerate man and one who thought of everything. Not only had he stocked his Lear with a splendid variety of liquor, liqueurs, wines, and beers, he'd provided an exceptionally attractive stewardess to serve them up. His three hired men—Hamilton, Hiller, and Serrano—had long cold drinks in their hands. Hamilton gazed happily at the green immensity of the Amazonian rain forest passing by below.

"This beats hacking your way through that lot down there," he said. He looked round the cabin of the luxuriously appointed jet. "But this tube is for the carriage trade. What transport is Smith thinking of using when we make our trip into the Mato Grosso?"

"No idea," Hiller said. "Matters like that, Smith doesn't consult me. He's got his own advisers for that. You'll be seeing him in a couple of hours. I suppose he'll tell you then."

"I don't think you quite understand," Hamilton said, in an almost gently explanatory tone. "I only asked what transport he was *thinking* of using. Any decisions he and his experts have made are not really relevant."

Hiller looked at him in slow disbelief. "*You* are going to tell *him* what we're to use?"

Hamilton beckoned the stewardess, smiled, and handed over his glass for a refill. "Nothing like savoring the good life—while it lasts." He turned to Hiller. "Yes, that's the idea."

"I can see," Hiller said heavily, "that you and Mr. Smith are going to get along just fine."

"Oh, I hope so, I hope so. You said we'd be seeing him in two hours. Could you make it three?" He looked disparagingly at his wrinkled khakis. "These look well enough in Romono, but I have to see a tailor before I go calling on multimillionaires. You say we're being met when we arrive. Think you can drop me off at the Grand?"

"Jesus!" Hiller was clearly taken aback. "The Grand—*and* a tailor. That's expensive. How come? Last night in the bar you said you had no money."

"I came on to some later."

Hiller and Serrano exchanged looks. Hamilton continued to gaze placidly out of the window.

As promised, a car was waiting at the private airport in Brasilia. "Car" was too mundane a word to describe the stretched, customized, maroon Rolls, big enough to accommodate a football team. In the back it had a television receiver, a bar, and an ice maker. Up front—far up front—were two uniformed men in olive-green livery. One drove the car: The other's main function in life appeared to be opening doors when the passengers entered or left. The engine, predictably, was soundless and so was the clock in the dash. If it were part of Smith's

pattern to awe visitors, he succeeded in the case of
Serrano. Hamilton appeared to be unimpressed,
possibly because he was busy inspecting the bar. He
was disappointed: Somehow Smith had overlooked
providing a stewardess for the rear of the Rolls.

They drove through the wide avenues of that
futuristic city and pulled up outside the Grand
Hotel. Hamilton dismounted—the door having
been magically opened for him, of course—and
passed swiftly through the revolving door. Once
inside, he looked out through the glassed-in porch.
The Rolls, already more than a hundred yards
away, was turning a corner to the left. Hamilton
waited until it had disappeared from sight, left by
the revolving door, and started to walk briskly back
in the direction from which they had come. He
gave the impression of one who knew the city, and
he did: He knew Brasilia very well indeed.

Five minutes after dropping Hamilton the maroon Rolls pulled up outside a photographer's shop.
Hiller went inside, approached a smiling and affable
assistant and handed over the film that had been
taken from Hamilton.

"Have this developed and sent to Mr. Joshua
Smith, Villa Haydn." There was no need for Hiller
to add the word "immediately." Smith's name guaranteed immediacy. Hiller went on. "No copy is to
be made of these transparencies and neither the
person who develops them nor any other member
of your staff is ever to discuss it. I hope that is
clearly understood."

"Yes, sir. Of course, sir." The smile and the affability had vanished to be replaced by total obsequiousness. "Speed and secrecy. Those are guaranteed, sir."

"And perfect prints?"

"If the transparencies are perfect, so will any prints be."

"All right. For now, I'll take the best slides you can produce—in a hurry." Hiller couldn't think of how else he could threaten the now thoroughly apprehensive assistant so he nodded and left.

Eleven minutes later, Hiller and Serrano were in the drawing room of the Villa Haydn. Serrano was seated, as were Tracy, Maria Haller, and a fourth and as yet unidentified man. Smith said he wanted to talk to Hiller somewhat apart—"somewhat apart" in that huge drawing room meant a considerable distance—and they did, glancing occasionally in Serrano's direction.

Hiller said, "Of course, I can't vouch for him. But he knows an awful lot that we don't, and I can always see to it that he makes no trouble. Come to that, so would Hamilton. Hamilton has a rough way of dealing with people who step out of line." Hiller went on to tell the sad tale of Serrano's mugging.

"Well, if you say so, Hiller." Smith sounded doubtful, and if there was one thing Smith didn't like it was being doubtful about anything. "You certainly haven't let me down so far." He paused.

"But your friend Serrano seems to have no history, no past."

"Neither have most men in the Mato Grosso. Usually because they have too much of a past. But he knows his jungle—and he knows more Indian dialects than any man around here except maybe Hamilton. Certainly more than any man in the Indian Protection Service."

"All right." Smith had made up his mind and seemed relieved for that. "And he's been close to the Lost City. Could be a useful backup man."

Hiller nodded toward the unidentified person, a tall, heavily built, darkly handsome man in his mid-thirties.

"Who's that, Mr. Smith?"

"Heffner. My chief staff photographer."

Hiller said, "Mr. Smith!"

"Hamilton would think it extremely strange if I didn't take a photographer along on such a historic trip," Smith said reasonably. He smiled. "I will confess, though, that Mr. Heffner can use one or two instruments other than his cameras."

"I'll bet he can." Hiller looked at Heffner with even closer interest. "Another with or without a past?"

Smith made no answer. A phone rang. Jack Tracy, who was nearest to it, walked across the room and picked it up, listened briefly, and replaced the receiver.

"Well, well. Surprise, surprise. The Grand Hotel has no one registered under the name of Hamilton.

Not only that, no member of the staff can recall ever seeing a man answering to the description."

Hamilton, at that moment, was in a lavishly furnished suite in the Hotel Imperial.

Ramon and Navarro, seated on a couch, were admiring Hamilton, who was admiring himself in front of a full-length mirror.

"Always did fancy myself in a fawn seersucker," Hamilton said complacently. "Don't you agree? This should knock Smith's eye out."

"I don't know about Smith," Ramon said, "but in that outfit you'd terrify even the Muscias. So no trouble with getting the invitation?"

"None. When he saw me flashing those gold coins in public he must have panicked in case some-one else would step in fast. Now, I'm pleased to say, he's convinced he's got me hooked, like some Goddamn fish."

"You still think that gold hoard exists?" Navarro said.

"I'm convinced it *did* exist. Not that it *does*."

"Then why did you want those coins?"

"When this is over they will be returned and the money reimbursed—all except the two that are now in the hands of Curly, our friend the head barman. But those were necessary. Speaking of fish, the shark, as we know, took the bait."

"So, no hoard, huh Señor?" Ramon said. "Disappointing."

"There is a hoard and a huge one. But not of those coins. Perhaps melted down, although that's unlikely. What's more likely is that it's been split up into private collectors' hands. If you want to dispose of an art treasure, be it a stolen Tintoretto or a Penny Black, then, as I don't have to tell you, Brazil is *the* place in the world. The number of Brazilian millionaires who spend hours in their air-conditioned, humidity-controlled, burglarproof, deep underground cellars gloating over stolen old masters boggles the imagination. Ramon, there's a wet bar right behind you, and I'm developing a sore and thirsty throat from lecturing callow youngsters on the facts of criminal life."

Ramon grinned, rose, and brought a large whiskey and soda to Hamilton and a soda each for himself and his brother. The twins never drank anything stronger.

Having eased his throat, Hamilton said, "What did you get on J. Smith?"

"Nothing more than you expected," Ramon said. "The number of companies he controls can't be counted. He's a financial genius. Charming and courteous, totally ruthless in his business dealings. By any reckoning, the richest man in the southern hemisphere. A sort of Howard Hughes in reverse. About Hughes's early days everything was known in detail, but the latter part of his life was so wrapped in mystery that many people who should have been in a position to know could scarcely believe that he had died on the flight from Mexico to the States, having been firmly convinced that he had died many years previously. Smith? Dead opposite. His past is a closed book and he never talks about it: Neither do any of his colleagues, friends, or supposed intimates—no one really knows whether he *has* any intimates—for the good reason that none of them was around in his early days. Today, his life . . . what do you say, is an open book? He conceals nothing and operates in a totally straightforward fashion. Any one of the shareholders in his companies can inspect the firm's books whenever they wish. He appears to have absolutely nothing to hide. I guess that when you are as brilliant as he is there's no point in being dishonest. After all, what's the point in it if you can make more money being honest? Today he knows everybody's business and lets anyone who wishes know all about his businesses."

"He's got something to hide," Hamilton said. "I know he has."

Navarro said, "What?"

"That's what we're going to find out, isn't it?" Hamilton said.

"I wish you wouldn't play your cards so close to your chest," Navarro said.

"What cards?"

He grinned. "And if we don't get back to work soon, I'll be asking, 'What chest?' "

"We look forward to watching you at work, Señor," Ramon said. His tone was neutral to the point of being ambiguous. "It should be worth watching. By every account, our man is above suspicion. He goes everywhere, sees everyone, knows everyone. And everyone knows that he and the President are blood brothers."

The President's blood brother was leaning forward in a chair in his splendid drawing room, oblivious of the company around him, staring at the silvered screen. The room had been so efficiently darkened by the heavy drapes that he would have had difficulty in seeing those around him. Even so, had it been broad daylight, he still wouldn't have seen them. His absorption was total.

The transparencies were of superb quality, taken with a sophisticated camera by a photographer who knew precisely what he was about. The color was true, the clarity and the resolution impeccable. And the projector the best that Smith's money could buy.

The first group showed a ruined and ancient city impossibly clinging to the top of a narrow plateau with, at the far end, a breathtakingly well-preserved ziggurat, as imposing as the best surviving works of the Aztecs or the Mayans.

A second group showed one side of the city perched on the edge of a cliff that dropped vertically to a river with the rain forest beyond. The third group showed the other side of the city overlooking a similar gorge with a river sliding swiftly past, suggesting its distant depths. A fourth group, clearly taken from the top of the hills, showed a reverse view of the ancient city, with a brief glimpse of scrubland beyond—once obviously terraced for cultivation—and with the two cliffsides meeting in the

middle distance. A fifth group, obviously taken 180°
from the same position, showed a flat, grassy plateau, the sides curving to meet like the bows of a
boat. Nearly incredible as those pictures were, the
next few groups were staggering.

They were taken from the air and, as transparency succeeded transparency, it became evident
that they, like a number of the previous ones, could
only have been taken from a helicopter.

The first of those helicopter shots showed the
entire ruined city from above. The second, from
perhaps five hundred feet higher up, showed that
the city was perched on top of a vertically sided,
boat-shaped pinnacle of rock splitting a river that
swept by on either side of it. Both arms of the river
were rock strewn, foaming white, clearly unnavi-
gable. Those taken from an even higher altitude
were a shock: Taken horizontally, they showed pictures of a densely crowded rain forest, reaching out,
it seemed, almost to touch the camera and extend-
ing, unbroken, to the distant horizon. Another set,
shot vertically, downward, made it clear that the
great outer cliffs walls of the twin gorges were at
least several hundred feet higher than the top of
the cliff walls that formed the island on which the
Lost City was built. The next group, taken at a still
higher elevation, showed a narrow gap between two
great stretches of forest reaching toward each other,
with the Lost City just vaguely visible in the gloomy
depths below. The last group, taken anywhere between five hundred and a thousand feet higher up

again, revealed nothing but the continuous majestic sweep of the Amazonian rain forest, unbroken from pictorial horizon to pictorial horizon.

It was small wonder, then, that the planes of the Brazilian ordnance survey services, whose pilots claimed, rightly, to have crisscrossed every square mile of the Mato Grosso, had never discovered the site of the Lost City. It just could not be seen from the air at ordinary plane altitudes. But the ancients, stumbling across it, had discovered the most invisible, the most inaccessible, the most impregnable fortress ever created by nature or devised by man.

The viewers in the Villa Haydn drawing room had sat throughout in silence. They knew they had seen something that no white man, with the exception of John Hamilton and his helicopter pilot, had ever seen before, something, perhaps, that no one had ever seen for generations, maybe even for centuries. They were hard people, tough people, cynical people, people who counted value only in the terms of cost, people conditioned to disbelieve, almost automatically, the evidence of their own eyes. But there is yet to be born a man or woman the atavistic depths of whose soul cannot be touched by that one questing finger that will not be denied, that primitive ancestral awe inseparable from watching the veil of unsuspected history being swept aside.

The slowly comprehending silence stretched out for at least a minute. Then, almost inaudibly, Smith exhaled his breath in a long sigh.

"Son-of-a-gun," he whispered. "Son-of-a-gun. He found it."

"If your intention was to impress us," Maria said, "you've succeeded. What on earth was that? And *where* is it?"

"The Lost City." Smith spoke absently. "Brazil. In the Mato Grosso."

"The *Brazilians* built pyramids?"

"Not that I know of. May have been some other race. Anyway, they're not pyramids, they're— Tracy, this is more in your field."

"Well. Not really my field either. One of our magazines commissioned an article on such so-called pyramids and I spent a couple of days with the writer and photographer on the job. Curiosity only, and wasted curiosity—I didn't learn much. Pyramid-shaped, sure, but those step-sided and flat-topped structures with exterior spiral steps or ramps are called ziggurats. No one knows where they originated, although it is known that the Assyrians and Babylonians had them. Oddly enough, this style bypassed Egypt, the virtually neighboring country. But it turned up again in ancient Mexico where you can still see some. Archaeologists and such like use this as a powerful argument for the idea of prehistoric contact between east and west. The only sure fact is that their origins are lost— lost in the mists of those prehistoric times. But this"—he waved at the screen—"this is going to drive the poor archaeologists up the wall. A ziggurat in the Mato Grosso."

* * *

"Ricardo?" Hamilton said. "I'll be leaving our friend's place in about two hours. Be driving— moment . . ." He broke off and turned to Ramon, lounging on the couch in the Imperial suite. "Ramon, what'll I be driving?"

"Black Cadillac."

"A black Cadillac," Hamilton said into the phone. "I don't wish to be followed. Thank you."

FOUR

THERE WERE SIX PEOPLE IN Joshua Smith's drawing room that sunny afternoon —Smith, Tracy, Maria, Hiller, Serrano, and Hamilton. All had glasses in their hands.

"Another?" said Smith. His hand reached out to touch the button that would summon the butler.

Hamilton said, "I'd rather talk."

Smith raised an eyebrow in slight if genuine astonishment. Not only had he heard from Hiller of Hamilton's reputation as a hard drinker, but his slightest suggestion was usually treated as a royal command. He withdrew his hand from the buzzer.

"As you wish. So we are agreed on the purpose of our visit. I tell you, Hamilton, I have done many things in the past that have given me a great deal of pleasure, but I've never been so excited—"

73

Hamilton interrupted him, something no one eve did to Smith. "Let's get down to details."

"By God, you *are* in a hurry. I'd have though that after four years—"

"It's a lot longer than that. But even after only four years a man starts to become a little impatient. He pointed toward Maria and Tracy. "Who are they?"

"We all know your rough-diamond reputation Hamilton." When Smith chose to use a cold tone he could do so most effectively. "But there's no need to be rude."

Hamilton shook his head. "Not rude. Just a man as you observed, in a hurry. I like to check on the company I'm keeping. As you do."

"As I do?" Again the eyebrow. "My dear fellow, if you would kindly explain—"

"And that's another thing," Hamilton said. That made it twice in thirty seconds that Smith had been interrupted, which must have constituted some sort of record. "I don't like being condescended to. I am not your dear fellow. I am not anybody's dear fellow. As *you do,* I said. Check up. Or perhaps you don't know the identity of the person who rang the Grand Hotel to see if I was actually staying there?"

It was a guess, but in the circumstances a safe one, and the flickered glance between Smith and Tracy was all the confirmation Hamilton required. He nodded toward Tracy.

"See what I mean?" Hamilton said. "That's the nosy bastard. Who is he?"

"You would insult my guests, Hamilton?" Smith's tone was now positively arctic.

"I don't much care who I insult—or should I say whom'? He's still a nosy bastard. Another thing, when I ask questions about people I do it honestly and in the open, not behind their backs. Who is he?"

"Jack Tracy," Smith said stiffly, "is the managing director of McCormick-Mackenzie International Publications Division." Hamilton looked unimpressed. "Maria is my confidential secretary and, I might add, a close personal friend."

Hamilton looked away from Tracy and Maria almost as if he had already dismissed them from his mind. "I'm not interested in your relationships. My fee."

Smith's face showed his conviction that gentlemen did not discuss business in this crude and abrupt fashion. Momentarily, his expression hovered between astonishment and anger. Many years had passed since any man had dared talk to him in such a way. It visibly required considerable willpower to repress his anger.

"Hiller mentioned it, I think," Smith said. "A six-figure sum. One hundred thousand dollars. U.S. dollars, friend."

"You don't get the idea. I'm not your friend. A quarter million."

"Ludicrous."

"Okay. I could say, 'Thanks for the drink,' and walk out. I'm not childish. I hope you're not either.

Smith had not become the man he was without the ability to make his mind up rapidly. Without in any way appearing to capitulate he capitulated immediately.

"A man would want an awful lot of service for money like that."

"Let's get our terms clear. You get cooperation not service. I'll return to this point later. My fee is far from excessive in view of the fact that I'm damned certain you're in this not just to get a few nice photographs and a human-interest story. Whoever heard of Joshua Smith engaging upon an enterprise where money was not the prime and motivating factor?"

"As far as the past is concerned, I would agree with you." Smith's voice was quiet. "In this particular instance money is not the principal factor.

Hamilton nodded in acknowledgment. "That could well be. In this particular instance I might even believe you." Smith recognized Hamilton's concession and suppressed surprise, not entirely successfully. Then his expression changed to one of speculation. Hamilton smiled. "You're trying to figure out what I've figured that other motivation is. Don't concern yourself. It in no way concerns me. Now, transportation?"

"What? What was that?" Smith had been caught

off-balance by the sudden switch in topic, which he should not have been; it was a favorite tactic of his. "Ah! Transportation."

"Yes. What kind of transportation—air and water, we can forget land—do your companies have available?"

"A great deal, as you can imagine. What we don't have we can rent, although I should think the need would be unlikely. Tracy has all the details. Tracy, by the way, is both a qualified airplane and helicopter pilot."

"Helps. Where are the details?"

"Tracy?" Smith said this in such a way as to convey the impression that he was not the man to be concerned with details; he was famous for his gift of picking topflight lieutenants, delegating the bulk of the executive work to them, paying them well, being demanding, testing them, firing them. Survivors were sturdy. Tracy, who had been following the conversation closely, rose, crossed to where they were standing, and handed Hamilton a folder. The expression on Tracy's face bespoke a marked lack of affection: Managing directors do not take kindly to being called nosy bastards. Hamilton appeared not to notice.

He took the folder, read rapidly through the contents, pausing briefly now and again as something in particular caught his attention, then closed the folder. One had to assume that Hamilton had already absorbed the contents. For once, he seemed fairly impressed.

"Quite an air/sea fleet. Everything from a Boeing 727 to a Piper Comanche. Double-rotor freight helicopter—this is a Sikorsky Skycrane?"

"Yes."

"And a hovercraft. Can the helicopter lift the hovercraft?"

"Naturally," Tracy said. "That's why it was brought.".

"Where's the hovercraft? Corrientes?"

Smith said, "How the hell do you know?"

"Logic. Wouldn't be much good to you here or in Rio, would it? I'll take this folder. See you this evening."

"This evening?" Smith looked unhappy. "Damn it man, we have to draw up our plans and—"

"I'll draw up the plans. I'll explain them when I return with my assistants this evening."

"Damn it all, Hamilton, *I* am putting up all the money. The man who pays the piper calls the tune."

"This time out, you're second fiddle."

Hamilton left, leaving behind him a brief but profound silence. Tracy said, "Of all the arrogant, hard-nosed, intransigent bastards—"

"Agreed, agreed," Smith said. "But he holds the cards, all of them." He looked thoughtful. "For the moment, enigma. Rough, tough, but dresses well, speaks well, obviously at home in any territory. Nuances, clever nuances. At ease in my drawing room. Not many strangers are. Come to that, nobody is."

Tracy said, "And he's come to the conclusion

that this lost city is so dangerously inaccessible that he's not prepared to try the same route again. So— a helicopter. Or hovercraft."

"I wonder." Smith was still looking thoughtful. "Why else would a man like that throw in his lot with us?"

"Because he's convinced he can eat us alive," Maria said. She paused. "Maybe he will at that."

Smith looked at her without expression, then crossed to the dining-room window. Hamilton was just moving away in his Cadillac. A man stopped polishing a nondescript Ford, glanced toward Smith's window, nodded, climbed into his car, and followed the Cadillac.

Hamilton was driving down one of Brasilia's broad boulevards. He consulted his rearview mirror. The Ford was about two hundred yards behind. Hamilton increased his speed. So did the Ford. Both cars were now traveling well above the speed limit. A police car appeared behind the Ford, switched on the siren, overtook, and flagged the Ford to a stop.

The Ministry of Justice was a splendid building, and the large airy office in which Hamilton sat opposite across a polished leather table from Colonel Ricardo Diaz was suitably sumptuous. Diaz, in an immaculately cut uniform, was large, tanned, and looked competent to a degree, which he was. Diaz took a sip of some indeterminate liquid and sighed.

"About Smith, Mr. Hamilton, you know as much as we do—everything and nothing. His past is a mystery, his present an open book that anyone is welcome to read, as everyone says. It is just that the dividing line between the present and the past is not exactly known. It is known that he appeared— or, rather, emerged or surfaced in Santa Catharina, a province with a traditionally heavy Germanic settlement, in the late forties. Whether he is of similar origin is not known: His English is as immaculate as his Portuguese, but as far as is known, he has never been heard to speak German.

"His first business venture was to produce a newspaper aimed primarily at the native German speakers in the province but printed in Portuguese. It was conservative and strongly pro-establishment and marked the beginning of a long and close association with the government of the time, an association that has persisted, despite changes of government, to this day.

"He then branched out into the fields of plastics and ball-point pens. Smith was never an innovator —he was and remains a takeover specialist and a share manipulator of genius. Both the publishing and the industrial sides of his businesses expanded at a remarkable speed, and within ten years he was, by any standards, a very wealthy man."

Hamilton said, "He couldn't have been without the odd cruzeiro to begin with."

"Agreed. Expansion on a scale such as Mr. J. Smith's must have called for a great deal of capital."

"And the source of capital is unknown?"

"Totally. But that's nothing to hold against any man. In this country—as in many others—we don't care to enquire too closely into those things.

"Now we come to Tracy. He is, as he claims, the general manager of Smith's publication division. Very tough, very able, nothing known about him in the criminal line, which could mean that he's either honest or very clever, for there is more than a manager here. The best you can say of him is that he's a soldier of fortune. The police are certain that the bulk of his activities are illegal—diamonds have an odd habit of disappearing when he's in the neighborhood—but he's never been arrested, far less convicted. Serrano is a small-time crook, not too bright, and a coward."

"He can't be all that cowardly if he ventures alone into the rain forests of the Mato Grosso. Not many white people would."

"That thought, I admit, also occurred to me. I'm merely passing on reported reputation, accuracy not guaranteed. Now, Heffner. Mr. Heffner's the joker. Wouldn't recognize a camera if he tripped over one. Well known to the New York police. Associated with crimes of violence and alleged gangland killings, but he's always, as you say, beaten the rap. Not too surprising really—no police in any country are going to come over all zealous and excited when one hoodlum dispatches another. Curious fellow. Usually well-spoken and civilized enough—look at those pillars of society, the Mafia bosses—but the veneer vanishes when he gets next to a bottle of Bourbon. And he has a weakness for Bourbon."

"And all this leaves Smith unaffected?"

"Nothing known against him, as I said, but you can't associate with characters like Hiller, Heffner, and Tracy without some tar rubbing off. Could well be the other way round, of course." He looked up as a knock came at the door. "Come in, come in."

Ramon and Navarro entered. The twins were clad in khaki suits and smiling cheerfully. Diaz looked at them and winced.

"The famous Detective-Sergeant Herera and the famous Detective-Sergeant Herera. Or infamous. You are far from home, gentlemen."

"Señor Hamilton's fault, sir." Ramon spread his hands apologetically. "He's always leading us astray."

"Mary's little lambs. Ah, Major."

A young officer entered and unrolled on the table a map of southern Brazil. It was marked with legends of varying kinds. Colored flags in circles and squares indicated different tribes, races, and languages. Other symbols indicated the state of hostility or friendliness of the tribes.

The major said, "This is the most up-to-date picture the Indian Protection Service can give you. There are some places, you understand, where even the Service do not care to investigate too closely. Most of the tribes are friendly—pacified, if you like. Some are hostile. Nearly always the white man's fault. A very few cannibal tribes. Those are known."

"And to be avoided, of course."

Hamilton pointed at a town on the map and looked at Diaz. "Corrientes. Smith has a hovercraft there—for obvious reasons. It's at the junction of the Paraná and Paraguay rivers, and he must be pretty sure the Lost City lies near the headwaters of one of those. I'm going up the Paraguay. I don't know it well, there may be bad rapids for all I know, but the helicopter can help if there are."

Diaz said, "Your friend has a helicopter?"

"My friend, as you call him, has got everything. This is a giant—a Sikorsky Skycrane. Well named —it can just about lift any damn thing. We'll base the helicopter at Asunción. The hovercraft can go up in three stages—to either Puerto Casado or Puerto Sastre in Paraguay, then into Brazil to Corumbá, then finally to Cuiabá. From there the helicopter can airlift it to Rio da Morte."

"And you would like to have some units of the Federal Army exercising near Cuiabá, is that it?"

"If it can be arranged."

"That has already been done."

"I am in your debt, Colonel Diaz."

"It would be more accurate to say that we are in your debt. If, that is to say—"

"*If* I come back?"

"Precisely."

Hamilton gestured toward the two young men.

"With the heavenly two to watch my back, what harm can befall me?"

Diaz looked at him briefly and doubtfully and pressed a button. An aide came in carrying a brown-leather case, extracted what looked to be a movie camera, and handed it to Hamilton, who squeezed a switch on the base. There came the faint whirring noise typical of an electric-powered camera.

Diaz said, "You won't believe this, but it will even take pictures if you wish."

Hamilton smiled but without humor. "I don't think I'll be indulging in any photography this time out. What's the transmitting range?"

"Five hundred kilometers."

"Enough. Waterproof?"

"Naturally. You leave tomorrow?"

"No. We have to get provisions and jungle gear and fly them to Cuiabá. We must get the hovercraft on the move. More important, though, I must go ahead and check on our friend 'Mr. Jones.' "

"Back to the Kolonie?"

"Back to the Kolonie."

Diaz said slowly, "You are an extraordinarily persistent man, Mr. Hamilton. God knows you've every right to be." He shook his head. "I fear for the health of your traveling companions in your forthcoming expedition. And for yours."

Hamilton had rejoined his traveling companions. Outside the uncurtained windows of the Villa Haydn's drawing room the sky was dark: The room

itself was brightly but not harshly lit by the light
from the three crystal chandeliers. There were nine
people in the room, most of them standing, most of
them with aperitif glasses in their hands. Present
were Hamilton, the twin Sergeants Herera, Smith
and his entourage. Heffner, to whom Hamilton had
just been introduced, was slightly flushed of face,
slightly loud of voice, and was sitting on an arm of
the chair Maria was occupying. Tracy was regard-
ing him with disfavor.

Smith said to Hamilton, "I must say your heavenly twins, as you call them, have an air of com-
petence about them."

"They're not much at home in drawing rooms.
But in the jungle, yes. They're good. Squirrel-
hunter's eyes."

"Meaning?"

"Either of them, with his rifle, can hit a playing
card at a hundred yards. Most people can't even
see a card at that distance."

"That meant to sound intimidating? Threaten-
ing?"

"Reassuring. Very useful accomplishment when
alligators or wild boars or wild people come at you.
Let's not confuse this coming trip with a senior
citizens' outing to the park."

"I'm aware of that." Smith was trying to sound
patient. "Well, your plan sounds reasonable. We
leave in a couple of days?"

"More like a week. You don't go into the Amazonian rain forest at a couple of hours' notice,

especially when you are going to be passing through hostile territory—and, believe me, we will be. We have to allow several days for the hovercraft to get up to Cuiabá—we don't know what difficulties it might encounter. Then we have to get all our provisions and equipment and fly them over to Cuiabá. At least, you will. I have some business to attend to first."

Smith raised an eyebrow. He was very good at raising eyebrows. "What business?"

"Sorry." Hamilton didn't sound sorry. "Where can one rent a helicopter in this city?"

Smith took a deep breath, then clearly made up his mind to ignore the outright rebuff. "Well, you know I have this freight Sikorsky—"

"That lumbering mill? No thanks."

"I have a smaller one. And a pilot."

"Again, no thanks. Tracy's not the only one who can fly a helicopter."

Smith looked at him in silence. His face was without expression but it was not difficult to guess what he was thinking: It would have been perfectly in keeping with Hamilton's nature—his policy of never letting his left hand know what his right was doing—to have flown his own helicopter over the Lost City, so that no other person could share his knowledge. To have shot those photographs himself *and* flown the chopper.

At last Smith said, "You're graciousness itself. You don't see a little friction arising when we set off on this search?"

Hamilton shrugged indifferently. "It isn't a search. I know where I'm going. And if you think some friction is going to arise, then why don't you leave behind those liable to give rise to friction? It's a matter of indifference to me who comes along, except for my own men."

"I'll decide that, Hamilton."

"Will you, now?" Again the same indifferent, infuriating shrug. "You like pictures, but in this case I don't think you've quite got the picture yet."

It was significant of Smith's perturbation that he actually went to the bar and poured another drink for himself. Normally, indeed invariably, he would have summoned his butler. Performing such a menial task gave him moments to compose himself.

He returned to Hamilton and said, "Another point. You're having your own way about making the plans—but we haven't yet decided who's going to be in charge of our little expedition, have we?"

"I have. I am."

Smith's impassive air now deserted him. He looked every inch the man he was reputed to be.

"Hamilton, I'm the paymaster."

"The ship owner pays his captain. Who's in charge at sea? Even more importantly, who's in charge in the jungle? You wouldn't last a day without me."

There was a silence in the room. The tension between the two men was all too obvious. Heffner rose from the arm of the chair, lurched once, and then crossed to where the two men were standing. The light of battle was in his truculent and bloodshot eyes.

"But, boss! You don't seem to understand." Heffner didn't speak the words, he sneered them. "This is the intrepid explorer himself. The one and only Hamilton. Haven't you heard? Hamilton is always in charge."

Hamilton glanced briefly at Heffner, then at Smith. "This is the kind of irritation I mean. Born to give trouble, bound for friction. What function does he perform?"

"My chief staff photographer."

"Looks like the artistic type. He coming?"

"Of course he is." Smith's tone was glacial. "Why on earth do you think Jack Tracy and I brought him down here?"

"I thought maybe he had to leave some place in a hurry."

Heffner took a step closer. "What's that mean, Hamilton?"

"Nothing new. I just thought that maybe your friends in the New York police department were beginning to take too close an interest in you."

Heffner stiffened momentarily; then he took another step forward. "I don't know what the hell you mean. You don't want to stop me, do you, Hamilton?"

"Stop you from coming along? Dear me, no."

Ramon looked at Navarro. Both men winced.

" 'S what I thought," Heffner said. "All you need is twenty pounds over another guy to make him see it your way."

"Provided, of course, that you're halfway sober."

Heffner gazed at him in alcoholic disbelief, then swung a roundhouse right at the side of Hamilton's head. Hamilton moved inside and brought up his own right in a deep jab as Heffner's ham fist swept harmlessly over his head. Gray-faced and doubled, Heffner sunk to his knees, his hands clutching his midriff.

Ramon said thoughtfully, "I think, Señor Hamilton, that he's halfway sober already."

"A short way with mutineers, eh?"

Smith was unmoved by the plight of his trusty chief photographer, and his irritation had given way to curiosity. "You seem to know something about Heffner?"

"I read the New York papers now and then," Hamilton said. "A little late when I get them, mind you, but that doesn't matter much. Heffner's news-making activities cover a fair period. What the Americans call a scofflaw. Involvement in various kinds of violence, gangland killings, that kind of stuff. He's cleverer than he looks, which I can't believe, or he has a clever lawyer. Anyway, he's always beaten the charges so far. It's impossible, of course, Mr. Smith, that you don't know this."

"I confess that there have been stories, rumors. I discount them. Two things. He knows his job, and a man is innocent until proved guilty." Smith paused and went on, "You know anything to *my* detriment?"

"Nothing. Everybody knows your life is an open book. A man in your position can't afford to have it otherwise."

"Me?" said Tracy.

"Don't want to hurt your feelings, Jack, but I never heard of you until this week."

Smith glanced down casually at a still prostrate Heffner, as if seeing him for the first time, and rang a bell. The butler entered. His face remained expressionless at the sight of the man on the floor: He had seen such things before.

"Mr. Heffner is unwell," Smith said. "Have him taken to his quarters. Dinner is ready?"

"Yes, sir."

As they left the drawing room Maria took Hamilton's arm. In a quiet voice she said, "I wish you hadn't done that."

"Don't tell me I've clobbered your fiancé?"

"My fiancé? I can't stand him. But he has a long memory—and a bad reputation."

Hamilton patted her hand. "Next time I'll turn the other cheek."

She snatched her hand away and walked quickly ahead of him.

Dinner over, Hamilton and his twin friends left in the black Cadillac. Inside its softness, Navarro said admiringly, "So now Heffner is labeled in their minds as the one you think is the bad apple in the barrel. Smith, Tracy, Hiller, and for all I know Serrano think that you think they are the driven snow. You really are a liar, Señor Hamilton."

"One really has to be modest about such skills, my man. Practice makes perfect."

FIVE

As DUSK APPROACHED, A HELI-copter, equipped with both floats and skids, set down on a sandy stretch on the left bank of the River Paraná. Both upriver and down, on the same bank, as far as the eye could see in the gloom, stretched the dense, dark rain forest. Except for the waterways, no opening in it could be seen. It was a wall. The far side of the river, the right or western bank, was invisible in the gathering gloom: At this point, close to where the River Iquelmi flowed into the Paraná, the parent river was more than five miles wide.

The helicopter cabin was dimly lit; the precaution had been taken of pulling black drapes across the windows. Hamilton, Navarro, and Ramon were having an evening meal of cold meat, bread, beer, and soda—beer for Hamilton, soda for the twins.

Ramon shivered theatrically. "I don't think I like this place."

"Not many people do," Hamilton said. "But it suits Brown—alias Mr. Jones—and his friends well enough. Defensively speaking, it's probably the most impregnable place in South America. Years ago I traced Brown and his fellow refugees to a place called San Carlos de Bariloche near Lake Ranco on the Argentine-Chilean border. God knows that was fortress enough, but he didn't feel secure even there, so he moved to a hideout in the Chilean Andes, then came here."

Navarro said, "He knew you were after him?"

"Yes. For years. Our wealthy friend in Brasilia has been after him for much, much longer. There may well be others."

"And now he no longer feels secure even here?"

"I'm almost certain he doesn't. I know he was in the Lost City this year, and several times in the past few years. But he likes his comforts and there are not many in that ruin. He may have taken a chance and returned. It's highly unlikely, but I have to check. Otherwise, there's no point in going to the Lost City.

"You have to have this confrontation between Brown and his friend."

"Yes. Otherwise, I have no proof. This—ah—meeting will give me all the proof I'll ever require."

"Remind me to take care of myself. I want to be alive to see it." Navarro turned and gazed at the curtain facing downstream. "It will not be easy to get into this place?"

"It will not be easy. Brown's estate here—it's known as Kolonie Waldner 555—is better guarded than the Presidential Palace. The estate is infested with trained guards—and when I say that I mean they're trained and proven killers. There's jungle to the north and south, dense as Heffner's head. Paraguay lies to the south, and Brown is a close friend of the President there. There's this river to the east, and a large number of German settlements—populated almost exclusively by ex-members of the S.S. —lie astride the roads to Asunción and Bella Vista. You won't even find a single river pilot here who is Brazilian born."

"No?"

"They're all Germans from the River Elbe."

Ramon said, "In view of what you've just told us, a thought occurs to me. How do *we* get in?"

"I'll admit I've given the matter some thought. Not too many options. There's a road used by supply trucks, but it's too long, too dangerous, and you have to pass through an armed gatehouse with electrified fences stretching away on both sides. There's also a landing stage about ten miles downriver from here—about fifteen miles north of the

Paraguayan border. The road up to the compound
is about a mile long and heavily patrolled. But it'
the only other way. At least there are no electrified
fences along the right bank of the Paraná—or ther
weren't the last time I was in there. We'll wait two
hours and move out."

"Would it be in order," Navarro said, "if we gave
you a look? What is known as a couple of old
fashioned, skeptical, are-you-crazy looks?"

"Help yourselves," Hamilton said agreeably.

He opened a rucksack, brought out three silenced
Lugers, three spare magazines, and three sheathed
hunting knives, and distributed them.

"Sleep if you can. I'll watch."

The helicopter, not under power, drifted with the
current down the right bank of the Paraná, keeping
as close inshore as possible to avoid the bright light
of a brilliant half moon riding high in a cloudless
sky. A door in the fuselage opened, a figure appeared, stepped down onto one of the pontoons,
and lowered an anchor quietly to the bed of the
river. A second figure appeared with a bulky pack-
age under his arm—there came a subdued hiss,
and within thirty seconds the rubberized dinghy was
fully inflated. A third man emerged from the fuselage carrying a small outboard motor and a medium-
sized battery. The first two men stepped gingerly
into the dinghy and took those items from him.
The engine was clamped onto the transom aft, the

battery lowered to the duckboard floor and coupled up to the engine.

The engine, once started, was almost soundless, and the southwest wind, the prevailing one in that area, carried what little noise there was upstream. The painter was unhitched from the helicopter and the dinghy moved downstream. The three occupants were crouched forward, listening intently and peering, not without some apprehension, into the gloom beneath the overhanging branches of the rain-forest trees.

A hundred yards ahead the river curved to the right. Hamilton switched off the electric motor, the twins dipped paddles into the water, and soon, a paddle occasionally touching the bank, they rounded the bend.

The landing stage, less than two hundred yards ahead, projected out into the river for a distance of twenty feet. Behind it, on land, there was a guardhouse that threw enough light to illuminate the cracked and splintered timber of the stage and two men, rifles shoulder-slung, maintaining a comfortable and relaxed guard on a couple of bentwood chairs. Both were smoking and they were sharing a bottle. They stood up as two other men came out from the guardhouse. They talked briefly, then the two relieving guards took over their chairs—and the bottle—while the previous guards went inside the guardhouse.

The dinghy grounded silently on the muddy bank

of the river and was secured by its painter to the low-hanging branch of a tree. The three men disembarked and disappeared into the undergrowth.

After they had gone about ten yards Hamilton said to Navarro in a barely audible whisper, "What did I tell you? No electrified fences."

"Watch out for the bear traps."

There were four men inside the guardhouse, all dressed in uniforms of the field-gray color used by the Wehrmacht in the Second World War. Fully clad, they were lying on camp beds: Three were asleep, or appeared to be. The fourth was reading a magazine. Some instinct—there was certainly no sound—made him glance upward and toward the doorway.

Ramon and Navarro were smiling benevolently at him. There was nothing benevolent, however, about the discouragingly steady Lugers held in their hands.

On the landing stage two guards were gazing out over the Paraná when someone cleared his throat, almost apologetically, behind them. They immediately swung around. Hamilton wasn't even bothering to smile.

Inside the guardhouse all six were securely bound beyond any hope of escape and were more than adequately gagged. Ramon looked at the two telephones, then questioningly at Hamilton, who nodded and said, "No chances."

Ramon sliced through the wires while Navarro started to collect the prisoners' rifles. He said to Hamilton, "Yes?"

Hamilton nodded. The three men left, threw the rifles into the Paraná, then began to move up the road connecting the landing stage with Kolonie 555. The twins pressed in closely to the forest on the left-hand side of the road while Hamilton kept to the right. They moved slowly, with the stealth and silence of Indians: They had long moved at will through the disaffected tribes of the Mato Grosso.

When they were only yards from the compound Hamilton waved his two companions to a halt. The compound of the Kolonie was well lit by the moon. It was built in the basic form of a barrack square and was perhaps fifty yards across. Eight huts faced onto this central square. Most of those were ramshackle, but one at the far left of the square was a solidly built bungalow. Close by that was an arched metal shed and, beyond that, a short runway. At the entrance to the compound, diagonally across the square from the bungalow, was a thatched hut that could well have been a guardhouse—a probability reinforced by the fact that a solitary figure leaned against the entrance wall. Like his colleagues on the landing stage he was in paramilitary uniform and carried a slung rifle.

Hamilton gestured to Ramon, who waved back. The three men vanished into the undergrowth.

The sentry, still leaning against the wall, had his head tilted back, a bottle to his lips. There came the

sound of a muffled blow, the sentry's eyes turned
up in his head, and three disembodied hands appeared from nowhere. One took the bottle from the
already powerless hand while the other two took
him under the armpits as he began to sag.

In the guardhouse six more men lay trussed and
gagged. Hamilton, alone in the middle of the room
and engaged in rendering rifles and pistols inoper-
able, looked up as Ramon and Navarro, each with
torch in hand, reentered the room, shaking their
heads. The three men left and began to move around
the other huts. As they passed by each one, Hamilton and Ramon remained outside while Navarro
entered. Each time Navarro emerged, shaking his
head. Finally, they arrived at the last building, the
solidly constructed bungalow. All three entered.
Hamilton, in the lead, found a switch and flooded
the room with light.

It was a combination office and living quarters,
devoid of people and furnished in considerable
comfort. Drawers and filing cabinets were carefully
searched—by turning everything upside down. But
they had nothing that interested Hamilton. They
moved on to another apartment, a bedroom, again
a very comfortable accommodation. Pride of place
was apparent and so too were three framed and
inscribed photographs on the walls—those of Hitler, Goebbels, and Stroessner, a former Paraguayan
President. The contents of the wardrobes were
sparse, indicating that the owner had removed the

bulk of the contents. In one cupboard stood a pair of brown riding boots. The Nazis had always insisted on black riding boots, despising brown ones as decadent: Stroessner, on the other hand, had favored brown.

From there the three moved into Brown's communication center, containing two large multicalibrated transceivers of the latest design. They located a toolbox, and while Hamilton and Ramon used chisels and screwdrivers to remove the faceplates and destroy the inner mechanisms, Navarro located all the spares and reduced them to scrap metal and shattered glass.

From there they moved on to the arched metal shed. It was a remarkable place: There ran down the middle of it what must have been the Kolonie's pride and joy, a genuine, full-length American bowling alley. Hamilton's men paid no attention to this. What attracted their attention and then their tools was a Piper Cub in a bay alongside the bowling alley. It took the men less than ten minutes to ensure that the Piper would never fly again.

On their way back to the Paraná, this time walking openly in the middle of the road, Ramon said, "So your friend *has* gone."

"In the inelegant phrase, the fat bird has flown the coop, taking most of his hard cases with him—Nazis, renegade Poles, renegade Ukrainians. As fine a collection of war criminals as you'll ever meet. Most of this bunch here belong strictly to the second division."

"Where do you think they've gone?"

"Let's ask, shall we?"

The three men entered the landing-stage guard-house. Wordlessly, they sliced the ankle bonds of one of the prisoners, removed his gag, dragged him to his feet, and led him outside down to the river edge.

Hamilton said, "Brown had three Piper Cubs. Where have the other two gone?"

The man seemed not to understand.

"Three *airplanes*," Hamilton snapped.

The guard spat in contempt. At a signal from Hamilton, Navarro cut the back of the guard's hand. The blood flowed freely. The guard was then led forward until he was teetering on the edge of the landing stage.

"Piranha," Hamilton said. "You know, fishy-fishy? Piranha can smell blood at a quarter of a mile. Ninety seconds and you'll be white bones, if a crocodile doesn't get you first. Either way . . ."

The guard looked in horror at his bleeding hand, dripping into the water. He was trembling. "North," he said. "North to Campo Grande."

"And after that?"

"I swear to God—"

"Throw him in."

"Planalto de Mato Grosso. That's all I know. I swear to you—"

Hamilton said wearily, "Stop your damned swearing. I believe you. Brown would never entrust real secrets to vermin."

Ramon said, "What do we do with the prisoners?"

"Nothing."

"But—"

"But nothing. I daresay someone will happen by and free them. Take this character inside and hobble and gag him."

Navarro looked doubtful. "It's a pretty deep cut. He could bleed to death."

"Oh, dear."

SIX

HAMILTON, RAMON, AND NAV-
arro were in a taxi moving along one of Brasilia's
broad boulevards. Ramon said, "This woman,
Maria, she comes?"

Hamilton looked at him and smiled. "She comes."

"There will be danger."

"The more, the better. Danger will at least help
to keep those clowns under control."

Navarro was silent for a moment, then he said
thoughtfully, "My brother and I hate all they stand
for. But you, Señor Hamilton, hate so much more."

"I have my reasons. But I don't hate them."

Ramon and Navarro looked at each other in lost
comprehension, then nodded as if in understanding.

A Rolls-Royce and a Cadillac had been backed
out of Smith's six car garage to make storage room
for what Smith regarded as being more important,

however temporarily, than the two cars. Hamilton, in the company of the eight peole who were going to accompany him, surveyed, with an uncritical eye, the extremely comprehensive layout of the most modern and expensive equipment necessary for survival in the Amazonian rain forests. He took his time about it, so much so in fact that one or two of the others were beginning to look, if not apprehensive, then at least uncomfortable. There is a law of nature that tycoons do not care to be kept waiting. Smith immediately proved that his patience was on a short fuse.

"Well, Hamilton? *Well?*"

"So. How the multi—or is it bulti?—millionaire travels into the boondocks. But good; really excellent."

Smith relaxed.

"There's one exception, though."

"Indeed? And what might that be?"

"Nothing missing, I assure you. Just some items surplus to requirements. Who are those guns for?"

"Us."

"No deal. Ramon, Navarro, and I carry weapons. You don't. None of you do."

"We do."

"Deal's off."

"Why?"

"You are children in the rain forests. No pop guns for kids."

"But Hiller and Serrano—"

"I admit they apparently know more than you do. That doesn't mean much. In the Mato Grosso they might even rate as adolescents. Forget what they've ever told you."

Smith lifted his shoulders, looked at the splendid armory of weapons he had assembled, then back at Hamilton. "Self-protection—"

"You've got no self-protection in there. We'll protect you. I don't want you all going around shooting harmless animals and innocent Indians. Even less do I like the prospect of being shot in the back when I've finally shown you where the Lost City is."

Heffner stepped forward. His fingers were actually clutching and unclutching, his face dusky with anger. "Look, Hamilton—"

"I'd rather not."

"*Stop it.*" Smith's voice was cold and incisive. But when he spoke again the tone had changed to one of bitterness and left no doubt that he was addressing Hamilton. "If I may say so, you have a splendid capacity for making friends."

"Oddly enough, I do. I have quite a few in this city alone. But before I make a man my friend I have to make sure he's not my enemy or potential enemy. Very sensitive about those things, I am. So's my back—sensitive, I mean, to having a knife stuck in it. I should know, I've had it done twice to me. I suppose I should have you all searched for flick knives or some such toys, but in your case I don't think I'll bother. The animals and Indians are safe. Frankly, I can't see any of you taking on an armed Indian or a jaguar with a penknife." He made a small gesture with his right hand, as contemptuous as it was dismissive, and from the sudden tightening and whitening of Smith's lips, it occurred to Hamilton, not for the first time, that Joshua Smith was easily the most dangerous man of them all.

Hamilton gestured again, this time toward the considerable pile of equipment lying on the garage floor. "How did those arrive—the packaging, I mean?"

"Crates. We crate them up again?"

"No. Too damned awkward to handle aboard a helicopter or hovercraft. I think—"

"Waterproof canvas bags." Smith smiled at the slight surprise on Hamilton's face. "We thought you might require something like that." He pointed toward two large cardboard boxes. "We bought them at the same time as we got the equipment. We're not mentally retarded, you know."

"Fine. Your plane, a DC-6, I understand—what's its state of readiness?"

"Superfluous question."

"I suppose. Where are the hovercraft and helicopter?"

"Almost at Cuiabá."

"Shall we join them?"

The DC-6 parked at the end of the runway of Smith's airfield may not have been in the first flush of youth but if the gleaming fuselage were anything to go by its condition was immaculate. Hamilton, Ramon, and Navarro, aided by an unexpectedly helpful Serrano, were supervising the loading of the cargo. It was a thorough, rigorous, painstaking operation. The supervision was intense. Each canvas bag in turn was opened, its contents removed, examined, returned, and the bag then sealed to make it waterproof. It was a necessarily lengthy and time-consuming process and Smith' patience was eroding rapidly.

He said sourly, "Don't take many chances, do you?"

Hamilton glanced at him briefly. "How did you make your millions?"

Smith turned and clambered aboard the aircraft.

After half an hour's flying time out from Brasilia the passengers, with the exception of Hamilton, were all asleep or trying to sleep. No one, it seemed, felt philosophical enough or relaxed enough to read: The clamor from the smooth-running but ancient engines was so great as to make conversation virtually impossible. Hamilton, as if prompted by instinct, looked around and his gaze focused.

Heffner, sprawled in his seat, appeared, from his partly opened mouth and slow deep breathing, to be asleep, a probability lent credence by the fact that his white drill jacket, carelessly buttoned, lay so as to reveal under his left armpit a white-felt container designed to accommodate the aluminum flask inside. This did not concern Hamilton: It was perfectly in character with the man. What did concern him was that on the other side of his chest could just be seen a small pearl-handled gun in a white-felt under-arm holster.

Hamilton rose and made his way aft to the rear

end of the compartment where the equipment, provisions, and personal luggage were stored. Hamilton didn't have to rummage around to find what he was looking for—when loading he had made a mental note of where every item was stored. He retrieved his rucksack, opened it, looked around to see that he was unobserved, removed a pistol, and thrust it into an inside pocket of his bush jacket. He replaced the rucksack and resumed his seat up front.

The flight to Cuiabá airport had been otherwise uneventful and so now was the landing. The passengers disembarked and looked around them in something like wonder, which was more than understandable as the contrast between Cuiabá and Brasilia was rather more than marked.

Maria, for one, was looking around in apparent disbelief. She said, "So *this* is the jungle. Quite, quite fascinating."

"This is civilization," Hamilton said. He pointed to the east. "The jungle's over there. That's where we'll be very soon, and once we get there you'd sell your soul to be back here." He turned and said sharply to Heffner, "Where do you think you're going?"

Heffner had been walking in the direction of the airport building. Now he stopped, turned, and looked at Hamilton with a languid, insolent air.

"Talking to me?"

"I'm looking at you, and I don't squint. Where are you going?"

"Look, I can't see it's any of your business, but I'm going to a bar. I'm thirsty. Any objections?"

"Every objection. We're all thirsty. But there's work to be done. I want all the equipment, food, and luggage transferred to that DC-3 there, and I want it done now. Two hours from now it will be too hot to work."

Heffner glared, then looked at Smith, who shook his head. Sullenly, Heffner retraced his steps and approached Hamilton, his face heavy with anger. "Don't be fooled by last time. Next time I'll be ready."

Hamilton turned to Smith and said, almost wearily, "He's your employee. Any more trouble or threats of trouble and he's on the DC-6 back to Brasilia. If you disagree, I'm on the plane back there. Simple choice."

Hamilton brushed contemptuously by Heffner, who stared after him with clenched fists. Smith took Heffner by the arm and led him to one side, clearly having trouble keeping his anger in check. He said, low-voiced, "Damned if I don't agree with Hamilton. Want to ruin everything? There's a time and a place to get tough, and this is neither the time nor the place. Bear in mind that we're entirely dependent upon Hamilton. You understand?"

"Sorry, boss. It's just that the bastard . . . My turn will come."

Smith was almost kind. "I don't think you understand. Hamilton regards you as a potential troublemaker—which, I have to say, you are—and he's the sort of man who will eliminate any potential source of trouble. God, man, can't you see? He's trying to provoke you so that he can have a reason, or at least an excuse, for disposing of you."

"And how would he do that?"

"Having you sent back to Brasilia."

"And failing that?"

"Don't talk about such things."

"I can take care of myself, Mr. Smith."

"Taking care of yourself is one thing. Taking care of Hamilton is another kettle of fish altogether."

They watched, some of them with evident apprehension, as a giant twin-rotored helicopter, cables attached to four lifting bolts, clawed its way into the air, raising a small hovercraft with it. The hovercraft's rate of climb was barely perceptible. At five hundred feet, it slowly began to move due east.

Smith said uneasily, "Those hills look mighty high to me. Sure they'll make it?"

"You'd better hope so. They're your machines." Hamilton shook his head. "Do you think the pilot would have taken off unless he knew it was in the cards? Only three thousand feet. No trouble."

"How far?"

"The headwaters of the Rio da Morte is only a hundred miles away. To reach the landing strip? Perhaps eighty. In half an hour's time we'll leave in the DC-3. We'll still be there before them."

Hamilton moved off and sat by the side of the river, idly lobbing stones into the dark waters. Some minutes later Maria appeared and stood uncertainly beside him. Hamilton looked up, then glanced away.

She said, "Is it safe to sit here?"

"Boyfriend let you off the leash?"

"He's not my boyfriend." She spoke with such vehemence that Hamilton looked at her quizzically.

"You could have fooled me. Misinterpretations, easy to come by. You have come, no doubt, or been sent to ask a few craftily probing questions?"

She said quietly, "Do you have to insult everybody? Wound everybody? Antagonize everybody? Provoke everybody? Back in Brasilia you said you had friends. It's difficult to understand how you have any."

Hamilton smiled. "Now look who's doing the insulting."

"Between gratuitous insults and the plain truth there's a big difference. I'm sorry to have disturbed you." She turned to walk away.

"Oh, come and sit down. Childish, childish. Maybe I can ask a few probing questions myself while you congratulate yourself on having found a chink in Hamilton's armor. I suppose that could be misinterpreted as an insult, too. Just sit down."

She looked at him doubtfully. "I asked if it's safe to sit here."

"A damn sight safer than trying to cross a street in Brasilia."

She sat down gingerly, a prudent two feet away from him. "Things can creep up on you."

"You've read the wrong books or talked to the wrong people. Who or what is going to creep up on us? Indians? There's not a hostile Indian within two hundred miles. Alligators, jaguars, snakes—they're

a damn sight more anxious to avoid you than yo
are to avoid them. There are only two dangerou
things in the forest—the *quiexada,* the wild boa
and the *carangageiros.* They attack on sight."

"The *caran* what?"

"Giant spiders. Great hairy creatures the size o
soup plates. They come at you one yard at a tim
Jumping, I mean. One yard and that's it."

"How horrible!"

"No problem. None in those parts. Besides, yo
didn't have to come."

"Here we go again." Maria shook her head. "Yo
really don't care much for us, do you?"

"A man has to be alone at times."

"Evasion, evasion." She shook her head agair
"You're always alone. Married?"

"No."

"But you were." It wasn't a question, it was
statement.

Hamilton looked at her, at the remarkable brow
eyes. They reminded him suddenly, painfully, o
the only pair he'd ever seen like them. "You ca
tell?"

"I can tell."

"Well, yes."

"Divorced?"

"No."

"No? You mean—"

"Yes."

"Oh! Oh, I am sorry. How—how did she die?"

"Come on. Plane to catch."

"Please. What happened?"

"She died violently."

"Accident?"

"No."

Hamilton stared out across the river, wondering hat had caused him to make this admission to a otal stranger. Ramon and Navarro knew, but they ere the only two in the world he'd told. Perhaps a inute passed before he became conscious of the ght touch of fingertips on his forearm. Hamilton irned to look at her and knew at once that she asn't seeing him: The big brown eyes were masked tears. Hamilton's first reaction was one of an lmost bemused incomprehension: This was totally ut of character with the image she—ably abetted y Smith—projected of herself as a worldly-wise, treet-wise, cosmopolitan.

Hamilton gently touched the back of her hand nd at first she didn't appear to notice. Perhaps alf a minute passed before she wiped her eyes with he back of her free hand, disengaged her other and, smiled apologetically, and said, "I'm sorry. Vhat must you think of me?"

"I think I may have misjudged you. I also think hat in some way, some time, you may have suffered lot."

She had nothing to say to this, just wiped her yes again, rose, and turned away.

"Battered" is the adjective invariably and usually nevitably applied to descriptions of vintage and uperannuated DC-3's, and this one was no excep-ion. If anything, it was an epitome, a prime exam-

ple of a battered life. The gleaming silver fuselage
of yesteryear was a fond and distant memory; the
metal skin was pitted and scarred and appeared to
be held together by large areas of rust. The engines,
when started up, were a splendid complement to
the rest of the plane, coughing, spluttering, and
vibrating to such an extent that it seemed improb-
able that they would not be shaken free from their
frame. But the plane lived up to its reputation as
one of the toughest and most durable ever built
With what seemed an arthritic Herculean effort—
it was underloaded—it clambered off the runway
and headed east into the late afternoon sky.

There were eleven people in the plane: Hamil
ton's party, the pilot, and co-pilot. Heffner, as was
customary, was taking counsel with a bottle of
scotch: The aluminum flask, presumably, was be
ing held as an emergency reserve. Seated across the
aisle from Hamilton, he turned to him and spoke
or, rather, shouted, for the rackety clamor from the
ancient engines was almost deafening.

"Wouldn't kill you to tell us your plans, would
it, Hamilton?"

"No, it wouldn't kill me. But what's it matter
How's that going to help you?"

"Curiosity."

"No secret. We land at Romono airstrip about
the same time as the helicopter and hovercraf
Helicopter refuels—even those big birds have only
a limited range—takes the hovercraft downstream
leaves it, returns, and takes us down to join it in
the morning."

Smith, sitting in the seat next to Hamilton and listening, put a cupped hand to Hamilton's ear and said, "How far downstream and why?"

"I'd say about sixty miles. There are falls about fifty miles from Romono. Not even a hovercraft could negotiate them, so this is the only way we can get it past there."

Heffner said, "You have a map?"

"As it happens, I have. Not that I need it. Why do you ask?"

"If anything happens to you, it would be nice to know where we are."

"You better pray nothing happens to me. Without me, you're finished."

Smith barked into Hamilton's ear, "You have to antagonize him? You *have* to provoke him?"

Hamilton looked at him, his face cold. "I don't have to. But it's a pleasure."

Romono airstrip, like Romono itself, looked, as it always did, a miasmic horror. Pilots found landing there a poor alternative to the jungle. The DC-3 and the helicopter-cum-hovercraft arrived on the strip within minutes of each other. The helicopter's rotor had hardly stopped when a small fuel tanker moved out toward it.

The passengers disembarked from the DC-3 and looked around. Their expressions ranged from incredulous to appalled.

Smith contented himself with saying merely, "Good God!"

"I don't believe it," Heffner said. "What a stinking dump. Jesus, Hamilton, this the best you could do?"

"What are you complaining about? Better than Forty-second Street." Hamilton pointed to the tin shed that constituted both the arrival and departure terminals. "Look at that sign there. ROMONO INTERNATIONAL AIRPORT. What's more reassuring than that? This time tomorrow, you may be thinking of this as home sweet home. Within three days, it'll be paradise. Enjoy it. Think of it as the last outpost of civilization." They groaned. "Look, as the poet says, your last on all things lovely every hour. Take what you need for the night. We have a splendid hotel here—the Hotel de Paris. Those who don't fancy it—well, I'm sure Hiller will put you up." He paused. "On second thought, I think I could have a better use for Hiller."

Smith said, "What kind of use?"

"With your permission, of course. You know that this hovercraft is the linchpin to everything?"

"I'm not a fool."

"The hovercraft will be anchored tonight in dicey waters. By which I mean that the natives on either side of the Rio da Morte range from the unreliable to the unfriendly to the downright hostile. So, it must be guarded. I suggest that this is not a task for one man, Kellner, the pilot, to do. In fact, I'm not suggesting, I'm telling you. Even if a man could keep awake all night, it would still be damned difficult. So, another guard. I suggest Hiller." He turned to Hiller. "How are you with automatic weapons?"

"I can find my way around."

"Fine." He turned back to Smith. "You'll find a bus waiting outside the terminal." He reboarded the plane and emerged two minutes later bearing two automatic weapons and some drums of ammunition. By this time Hiller was alone. "Let's go to the hovercraft."

Kellner was standing by his craft. He was thirty-ish, sun-tanned, tough.

Hamilton said, "When you anchor tonight, do it in midstream."

"There'll be a reason for that?" Kellner's Irish was up and was in his voice.

"Because if you tie up to either bank the chances are terrific that you'll wake up with your throat cut. Only, of course, you don't wake up."

"I don't think I'd like that." Kellner didn't seem unduly perturbed. "Midstream for me."

"Even there you won't necessarily be safe. That's why Hiller is coming with you—needs two men to guard against an attack from both sides. And that's why we have those two nasty little Israeli sub-machines along."

"I see." Kellner paused. "I'm not much sure that I care for killing helpless Indians."

"When those same helpless Indians puncture your hide with a dozen darts and arrowheads, all suitably poisoned, you might change your mind."

"I just changed it."

"Know anything about guns?"

"I was in the S.A.S. If that means anything to you."

"It means a great deal to me." The S.A.S. was

Britain's elite commando regiment. "Well, that saves me explaining those toys to you, I suppose."

"I know them."

"One of my luckier days," Hamilton said. "Well, see you both tomorrow. Anyhow, that's the plan."

The saloon of the Hotel de Paris, after closing hours, had six occupants. Heffner, glass in hand, was slumped in a chair, but his eyes were open: Hamilton, Ramon, Navarro, Serrano, and Tracy were asleep, or apparently so, stretched out on benches or on the floor. Bedrooms were, that night, at a premium in the Hotel de Paris. As they were all equally dreadful and bug-ridden, Hamilton had explained, this was not a matter for excessive regret.

Heffner stirred, stooped, removed his boots, rose and padded his noiseless way across to the bar, deposited his glass on the counter, then crossed silently to the nearest rucksack. Heffner opened it, searched briefly, removed a map, and studied it intently for some minutes before returning it to the rucksack. He returned to the bar, poured himself a generous measure of the Hotel de Paris' "scotch." He didn't know the label but scotch, he thought, was scotch. Wherever the birthplace of that brand, it wasn't in the highlands. He returned to his seat, replaced his shoes, leaned back in his chair to enjoy his nightcap, spluttered, and emptied half the contents on the floor.

Hamilton, Ramon, and Navarro, heads propped on hands, regarded him with a quietly speculative air.

Hamilton said, "What's the matter? Don't like the bar scotch? Aged in the bottle—two, three months sometimes."

Heffner spat.

"Well, did you find what you were looking for?"

Heffner didn't say whether he had or not.

"One of the three of us is going to keep an eye on you for the rest of the night, Heffner. You try to stir from that chair and I will take the greatest pleasure in putting you back in it, probably for good. I don't much care for people who meddle in my belongings."

Hamilton and the twins slept soundly throughout the night. Heffner did not once leave his chair.

=SEVEN=

JUST AFTER DAWN, THE HELICOP-
ter pilot, John Silver—generally known as Long
John—was at the controls. The party of nine em-
barked and stowed their overnight luggage with
the food and equipment that had been transferred
from the DC-3. Hamilton took the co-pilot's seat.
So cavernous was the interior of the giant helicopter that it seemed virtually empty. It rose effort-
lessly and flew easterly, paralleling the course of
the Rio da Morte. All the passengers had their
heads craned, peering through what few windows
there were: They were seeing for the first time the
true Amazonian rain forest.

Hamilton turned in his seat and pointed forward. "That's an interesting sight." His voice was a shout.

On a wide mud flat, perhaps almost a mile long, and on the left bank, scores of alligators lay motionless as if asleep.

"Good God!" It was Smith. "God! Are there so many 'gators in the world?" He shouted to Silver, "Take her down, man, take her down!" Then to Heffner, "Your camera! Quick!" He paused, as if in sudden thought, then turned to Hamilton. "Or should I have asked the expedition commander's permission?"

Hamilton shrugged. "What's five minutes?"

The helicopter came down over the river in great sweeping, controlled circles. Long John was clearly a first-rate pilot.

The alligators, hemmed in the narrow strip between forest and river, seemed to stretch as far as the eye could see. Depending upon one's point of view, it was a fascinating, horrifying, or terrifying spectacle.

Tracy said, almost in awe: "My word, I wouldn't care to crash-land among that lot."

Hamilton looked at him. "That's the least of the dangers down there."

"The least?" Smith said.

"This is the heart of the Chapate territory."

"That meant to mean something to me?"

"It would mean something to you if you ended up in one of their cooking pots."

Smith looked at him doubtfully, clearly not knowing whether to believe him or not, then turned to the pilot.

"That's low enough, Silver." He twisted in his seat and shouted at the top of his voice, "God's sake man, hurry."

"Moment, moment," Heffner bawled back. "There's such a damned jumble of equipment here."

There was, in fact, no jumble whatsoever. Heffner had already found his own camera, which lay at his feet. In Hamilton's rucksack he had found something that he had missed the previous night for the good enough reason that he hadn't been looking for it. He held a leather-bound case in his hand, the one Colonel Diaz had given to Hamilton. He extracted the camera from the case, looked at it in some puzzlement, then pressed an unfamiliar switch in the side. A flap fell down, noiselessly, on oiled hinges. His face registered at first bafflement, then understanding. The interior of the camera consisted of a beautifully made transistorized radio transceiver. Even more importantly it bore some embossed words in Portuguese. Heffner could read enough Portuguese to get by—especially official language. He read the words and his understanding deepened. The radio was the property of the Brazilian Defense Ministry—which made Hamilton a government agent. He clicked the flap in position.

"Heffner!" Smith had twisted again in his seat. "Heffner, if you—Heffner!"

Heffner, radio case in one hand and pearl-handled pistol in the other, approached. His face was a smiling mask of vindictive triumph. He called out, "Hamilton!"

Hamilton swung around, saw the wickedly smiling face, his camera-radio held high, and the pearl-handled pistol, and threw himself to the floor of the aisle, his gun coming clear of his bush jacket. Even so, despite the swiftness of Hamilton's movement, Heffner should have had no trouble disposing of Hamilton, for he had the drop on him and his temporarily defenseless target was only a few feet away. But Heffner had spent a long night of agony in the Hotel de Paris. As a consequence, his hand was less than steady, his reactions impaired, his coordination considerably worse.

Face contorted, Heffner fired twice. With the first came a cry of pain from the flight deck. With the second the helicopter gave a sudden lurch. Then Hamilton fired, just once, and a red rose bloomed in the center of Heffner's forehead.

Hamilton took three quick steps up the aisle and had reached Heffner before anyone else had begun to move. He stooped over the dead man, retrieved the camera-radio case, checked that it was closed, then straightened. Smith appeared beside him, a badly shaken man, and stared down in horror at Heffner.

"Between the eyes, between the eyes." Smith shook his head in total disbelief. "Between the eyes. Christ, man, did you have to do that?"

If he was upset, Hamilton had his distress well under control. "I tried to wing him, but the helicopter lurched. He twice tried to kill me before I pulled the trigger. I gave orders that no one was to carry guns. He's dead by his own hand."

The helicopter gave another and even more violent lurch, and although it still carried a good deal of forward momentum, seemed to be fluttering and falling from the sky like a wounded bird.

Hamilton ran forward, clutching at whatever he could to maintain his balance. Silver, blood streaming from a cheek wound, was fighting to regain control of the uncontrollable helicopter.

Hamilton said, "Quick! Can I help?"

"Help? Hell no. I can't even help myself."

"What happened?"

"First shot burned my face. Nothing. Superficial. Second shot must have gone through one or more hydraulic lines. Can't see exactly, but it can't have been anything else. What happened back there?"

"Heffner. Had to shoot him. He tried to shoot me, but he got you and your controls instead."

"No loss." Considering the circumstances, Silver was remarkably phlegmatic. "Heffner, I mean. But this machine is a different matter."

Hamilton took a quick look backward. The scene, understandably, was one of confusion and consternation although there were no signs of panic. Maria, Serrano, and Tracy, all three with almost comically dazed expressions, were sitting or sprawling in the central aisle. The others clung desperately to their seats as the helicopter gyrated through the sky. Luggage, provisions, and equipment were strewn everywhere.

Hamilton turned again and pressed his face close to the windscreen. The now pendulumlike motion of the craft was making the land below swing to and fro in a crazy fashion. The river was still directly beneath. The one plus factor appeared to be that they had now left behind them the mud flats where the alligators had lain in so lifeless a manner. Hamilton became suddenly aware that an island, perhaps two hundred yards long by half as wide lay ahead of them in the middle of the river, at a distance of about half a mile. It was wooded but not heavily so. Hamilton turned to Silver.

"This thing float?"

"Like a stone."

"See that island ahead?"

They were less than two hundred feet above the broad brown waters of the river: The island was about a quarter of a mile ahead.

"I can see it," Silver said. "I can also see all those trees. Look, Hamilton, control is close to zero. I'll never get it down in one piece."

Hamilton looked at him coldly. "Never mind the damned chopper. Can you get *us* down in one piece?"

Silver glanced briefly at Hamilton, shrugged, and said nothing.

The island was now two hundred yards distant.

As a landing ground it looked increasingly discouraging. Apart from scattered trees it was, but for one tiny clearing, thickly covered with dense undergrowth. Even for a helicopter in perfect health it would have made for an almost impossible landing site.

Some instinct made Hamilton glance to the left. Directly opposite the island, at about fifty yards and on the bank of the river, was a large native village. From the expression—or lack of it—on Hamilton's face it was clear that he didn't care for large native villages, or at least this particular one.

Silver's face, streaked with rivulets of sweat and blood, reflected a mixture of determination and desperation. The passengers, tense, immobile, gripped fiercely at any available support and stared mutely ahead. They, too, sensed what was about to happen.

The helicopter, swinging and side-slipping, weaved its unpredictable way toward the island. Silver was unable to bring the helicopter to the hover. As they approached this much-too-small clearing, the helicopter was still going far too fast. Its ground-level clearance was by then no more than ten feet. The trees and undergrowth rushed at them with accelerating speed.

Silver said, "No fire?"

"No fire."

"No ignition." Silver switched off.

One second later the helicopter dipped sharply,

crashed into the undergrowth, slid about twenty feet, and came to a jarring stop against the bole of a tree.

For a few moments the silence was complete. The engine roar had vanished. It was a silence compounded of the dazed shock caused by the violence of their landing and the relief of finding themselves still alive. Hamilton looked around. No one appeared to have sustained any serious injury.

Hamilton reached out and touched Silver's arm. "I'll bet you couldn't do that again, Long John."

Silver dabbed at his wounded cheek. "I wouldn't ever care to try." If he was in any way proud of his magnificent airmanship, it didn't show.

"Out! All out!" Smith's voice was a stentorian shout; he seemed unaware that normal conversational tones were again in order. "This can go up any moment."

"Don't be so silly." Hamilton sounded weary. "Ignition's off. Stay put."

"If I want to go out—"

"Then that's your business. Nobody's going to stop you. Later on, we'll bury your boots."

"What the hell does that mean?"

"A civilized interment of the remains. Maybe even those won't be left."

"If—"

"Look out your window."

Smith looked at Hamilton, then turned to the window, standing so as to achieve a ground view. His eyes widened, his lips parted, and his complex-

ion changed for the worse. Two alligators were
only feet from the helicopter, fearsome jaws agape,
their huge tails swinging ominously from side to
side. Wordlessly, Smith sat down.

Hamilton said, "I warned you before you left,
the Mato Grosso is no place for mindless little children. Our two leather-bound buddies out there are
just waiting for such children. And not only those
two. There'll be more around, lots of them. Also
snakes, tarantulas, and such. Not to mention—"
He broke off and pointed to the port windscreen.
"I'd rather you didn't have to, but take a look anyway."

They did as he asked. Among the trees on the
left bank could be seen a number of huts, perhaps
twenty in all with an especially large circular one
in the center. Several columns of smoke shimmered
up into the morning air. Canoes, and what looked
like a pinnace, fronted the village. A number of
natives, nearly naked, stood on the bank, talking
and gesticulating.

"But this is luck," Smith said.

"You should have stayed in Brasilia." Hamilton
sounded unwontedly sour. "Sure it's luck—the most
fiendishly bad luck. I see the chiefs are getting
ready."

There was a fairly long silence, then Maria said
almost in a whisper, "The Chapate?"

"None else. Complete, as you can now see, with
olive branches and calling cards."

Every one of the increasing number of natives

was now armed or was in the process of getting armed. They carried spears, bows and arrows, blow pipes, and machetes. The expressions on their face went well with the menacing gesticulations in the direction of the island.

"They'll be calling soon," Hamilton said, "and no for tea. Maria, would you give Mr. Silver a hand to fix up his face?"

Tracy said, "But we're safe here, surely? We have guns, plenty. They're carrying nothing that could penetrate our screens, far less the fuselage."

"True. Ramon, Navarro, get your rifles and come with me."

Smith said, "What are you going to do?"

"Discourage them. From crossing. Shame, really. They may not even know what a gun is."

"Jack makes sense," Smith said. "We're safe here. You *have* to be a hero?"

Hamilton stared at him until Smith looked un comfortable. Hamilton said, "Heroism doesn't en ter into it. Just survival. I wonder whether *you* would be halfway brave enough to fight for you own survival. I suggest you leave this to someone who knows how the Chapate wage war. Or do you want to be ready for immediate consumption when they get you?"

"What's that supposed to mean?" Smith tried to sound blustery, but his heart wasn't in it; his ego had been too severely dented.

"Just this. If they get as much as a foothold on this island the first thing they'll do is to set fire to he undergrowth and roast you alive in this metal offin."

There was a silence that lasted until Hamilton, Ramon, and Navarro had left the helicopter.

Ramon, the first to touch the ground, had his rifle on the nearest alligator immediately but the precaution proved needless: Both alligators immediately turned and scuttled away into the undergrowth.

Hamilton said, "Just keep an eye on our backs, Ramon."

Ramon nodded. Hamilton and Navarro moved toward the rear, took shelter behind the tail of the helicopter, and looked cautiously ashore.

A squat, powerfully built Indian dressed in a pink feather headdress, teeth necklace, a series of arm bracelets, and little else—definitely the chief—was ordering warriors into half a dozen canoes. He himself was standing on the bank.

Navarro looked at Hamilton, his reluctance plain. He said, "No choice?"

With equal regret Hamilton agreed, shaking his head.

Navarro lifted his rifle, aimed and fired in one swift motion. The report of the rifle momentarily paralyzed all activity on the bank. Only the chief moved: He cried out in pain and clutched his upper right arm. A second later, while the warriors were still immobilized in shock, another report was heard and another warrior struck in the same place. Navarro was a marksman of the most extraordinar accuracy.

Navarro said, "Not nice, Señor Hamilton."

"Not nice. As the old saying goes it's people lik us who have made people like them what they ar But this is hardly the time and place to explain tha to them."

Ashore the warriors rapidly abandoned the canoes and ran for the shelter of their huts and th forest, taking the two wounded men with then From those shelters they could be seen almost in mediately drawing bows and lifting blowpipes t their mouths. Hamilton and Navarro prudentl dropped behind cover as arrows and darts rattle and rebounded harmlessly off the fuselage. Navarr shook his head in sorrow and wonderment. "I'll be they've never even *heard* a rifle before. It is some thing less than a fair contest, Señor Hamilton."

Hamilton nodded, but made no comment fo comment would have been superfluous. After time he said, "That's all for now. I don't thin they'll try anything again before dark. But I'll kee watch—or arrange for others to do it. Meantim you and Ramon get rid of our four-legged friend and the creepy-crawlies. Try to chase them away shoo them away. If you have to shoot, for goodnes sake don't do it by the water's edge or in the wate Bath time tonight, and I don't want to attract ever piranha for miles around."

Hamilton reboarded the helicopter. Tracy saic

That was quite a hailstorm out there. Arrows and arts, I assume?"

"Didn't you see?"

"I wasn't too keen on looking. I'm sure those indows are made of toughened glass, but I wasn't oing to be the one to put them to the test. Poisned?"

"Certainly. But no curare, nothing lethal. They ave a less final but equally effective poison.

"What's it do?"

"Merely stuns. Too much curare affects the flavor f the stew."

Smith said sourly, "You certainly have a sum-ary way of dealing with the opposition."

"I should have negotiated? With brightly colored eads? Why don't you go and try it?" Smith said othing. "If you have any futile suggestions to offer, ither translate them into action or shut up. There's limit to the number of niggling remarks a man an take."

Silver, his face bandaged, intervened pacifically. And now?"

"A lovely long siesta until dusk. For me, that is. 'll have to ask you to take turns keeping watch. Jot only the village, but as far upstream and down-tream as you can see—the Chapate might con-emplate launching a canoe attack at some distance rom their village, although I consider it unlikely. If nything happens, let me know. Ramon and Navarro hould be back in twenty minutes. Don't bother etting me know."

Tracy said, "You place a great deal of faith
your lieutenants?"

"Total."

Smith said, "So we keep awake while you slee
Why?"

"Recharging my batteries for the night ahead

"And then?"

Hamilton sighed. "This helicopter, obvious
will never be airborne again. So we have to fi
some other means of rejoining the hovercraft, whi
I reckon must be about thirty miles downstream
We can't go by land. It would take us days to ha
our way down there and, anyway, the Chapa
would get us before we covered a mile. We need
boat. So we'll borrow one from the Chapate. There
a nice, big, and very ancient motor launch moor
to the bank there. Not their property for a certaint
The original owners were probably negotiated in
a pot long ago. And the engine will be a solid blo
of rust. Useless. But we don't need power to
downstream."

Tracy said, "And how do you propose we—ah—
obtain this boat, Mr. Hamilton?"

"I'll get it. After sunset." He smiled faintl
"That's why I intend a little sleep in advance."

Smith said, "You really do have to be a her
Hamilton, don't you?"

"And you'll really never learn, will you, Smit
No, I don't have to be a hero. I don't *want* to be
hero. You can go instead. You be the hero. Go o
Volunteer. Impress your girlfriend."

Smith slowly unclenched his fists and turned away. Hamilton sat and appeared to compose himself for slumber, oblivious of the dead Heffner laid now across the aisle from him. The others looked at one another in silence.

It was hours later, at dusk, when Hamilton said, "Everything packed? Guns, ammunition, last night's overnight bags, food, water, medicines? And, Long John, the chopper's two compasses might come in handy."

Silver indicated a box by his feet. "They're already in there."

"Excellent." Hamilton looked around him. "Well, that seems to be all. Heigh-ho."

"What do you mean 'that seems to be all,'" Smith said. He nodded toward the dead Heffner. "How about him?"

"Well, how about him?"

"You going to leave him here?"

"That's up to you." Hamilton spoke with almost massive indifference. He did not have to spell out his meaning. Smith turned and stumbled down the helicopter steps.

At the downstream end of the island, only Navarro, of all the party, was absent. In the gathering darkness Hamilton again checked all the packs. He seemed satisfied.

"There will be a moon," he said, "but it will be too late to save us. Moonrise is in about two and a half hours. When they attack—there's not much

'if' about it—it must be inside those two and a half
hours, which means it could be any time now, although I guess that they'll wait a bit until it is as
dark as possible. Ramon, join Navarro now. If they
attack before you get my signal, hold them off as
best you can for as long as you can. If my signal
comes first, get back here at once. Tracy?"

Tracy said, "I can tell you, I haven't been too
happy here for the past hour. No, no alligators. No
sign. Not a ripple. No gun?"

"Guns makes noises. Guns get wet."

Maria shivered and pointed to his big sheath
knife. "And that does neither?"

"Sometimes the first blow doesn't kill. Then there
can be a lot of noise. But no heroics. I don't expect
to have to use it. If I do, it means I've botched my
job."

Hamilton looked out across the river. The darkness had now deepened so that the shoreline was
no more than a dimly seen blur. He checked that the
coil of rope, the waterproof torch, and the sheath
knife were securely attached to his waist, walked
noiselessly into the river, and then slowly, silently,
began to swim.

The water was warm, the current was gentle, and
around him he could see nothing but the calm dark
water. Suddenly, he stopped swimming, trod water,
and stared ahead. He could see what he imagined
to be a tiny ripple in the black smoothness without
being able to see what caused it. His right hand
came clear of the water, clenched round the half of

his sheath knife. The tiny ripple was still there but even as he strained to watch it, it disappeared. Hamilton replaced the knife in its sheath. He wasn't the first person to have mistaken a drifting log for a crocodile, a considerably healthier sighting than the other way round. He resumed his silent swimming.

A minute later he drifted in toward the bank and caught hold of a convenient tree root. He straightened, paused, looked carefully around, listened intently, then emerged swiftly and silently from the river and disappeared into the forest.

A hundred yards brought him to the perimeter of the village. There were at least twenty native huts, haphazardly arranged, none showing any sign of life. In their approximate center was the much larger circular hut: Light could be seen through the numerous chinks in its walls. Ghostlike, Hamilton moved off to his right and moved round the perimeter of the village until he was directly to the rear of the large hut. Here he waited until he was sure— or as sure as he could possibly be—that he was alone, then moved forward to the rear of the hut. He selected a small lighted chink in the wall.

The communal hut was illuminated by some scores of tallow tapers. It was unfurnished. Dozens of natives were standing several deep round a cleared space in the middle where an elderly man was using a stick to make a diagram on the sand-covered floor while at the same time explaining something in an unintelligible tongue. The diagram was the outline of the island. Also shown was the

left bank of the river on which the village stood.
The speaker had drawn lines from the village, from
above the village, and from below the village, all
toward the island. A multipronged attack was to be
launched on the helicopter and its passengers. The
lecturer lifted his stick from time to time and
pointed it at various natives: It was apparent that
he was allocating canoe crews for their lines of
attack.

Hamilton moved away in the direction of the
upper riverbank, still circling the village. As he
passed the last hut, he stopped. At least twenty
canoes, some quite large, were tethered to the bank.
Almost at the end of the row, upriver, was the
dilapidated, paint-flaked motor launch, a little over
twenty feet in length. It was deep in the water but
floating so to that extent might be deemed river-
worthy.

Two Indian warriors, talking quietly, stood guard
at the downstream end of the row of canoes. As
Hamilton watched, one of them gestured toward
the village and walked away. Hamilton moved
around to one side of the hut and crouched there:
The Indian walked by on the other side.

Another problem arose, one that Hamilton could
do without. Even fifteen minutes ago he could have
remained where he had been and the remaining
Indian could have come within a few feet without
seeing him. Not anymore. The sun was gone, moonrise was still some time away, but, unfortunately,
the evening clouds, which earlier had so obligingly

offered concealment, had passed away and the southern skies were alive with stars. In the tropics stars
always seem much bigger and brighter than they
do in temperate climes. Visibility had become dis-
concertingly good.

Hamilton knew that the last thing he could
afford to do was to wait. He straightened and
advanced soundlessly, knife held in the throwing
position. The Indian was gazing out toward the
island, now easily visible. A shadow appeared
behind him and there came the sound of a sharp
but solid blow as the haft of Hamilton's knife caught
him on the base of the neck. Hamilton caught him
as he was about to topple into the water and lowered him none too gently to the bank.

Hamilton ran upstream. He came to the motor
launch, pulled out his signal torch, hooded the beam
with his hand, and shone it inside.

The launch was filthy and had at least four
inches of water in the bottom. The torch beam lit
on the centrally positioned engine which, as Hamilton had expected, was a solid block of rust. Floating, incongruously, were three cooking pans, obviously intended as bailers, at a guess the property
of some optimistic, now-departed missionaries. The
beam played swiftly around the entire interior of the
boat. There was no means of propulsion whatsoever:
no mast, no sail, no oars, not even a solitary paddle.

Hamilton straightened and moved quickly to examine some of the nearest canoes. Within a minute
he had collected at least a dozen paddles. He de-

posited those in the launch, hurried away, selected
two large canoes, and pulled them close to the
launch. He unwound the rope around his waist, cut
off two sections, and used those to tie the canoes in
tandem to the launch. He sliced through the manila
painter, pushed the launch into deeper water, scrambled in, seized a paddle, and began to move silently
away from the bank.

Paddling the launch—and its attendant canoes—
diagonally downstream, Hamilton was soon making
heavy weather of it. The launch was naturally cum-
berson and made more so by the amount of water
in it and Hamilton, able to use only one paddle, had
to switch continuously from side to side to keep it
on course. Briefly, he paused, located what he could
discern to be the upstream end of the island, now
almost directly opposite him, pulled out his torch
and pressed the button three times. He then pointed
his torch diagonally downstream and flashed again
three times. He replaced his torch and resumed
paddling.

Ashore, an Indian warrior emerged from the
communal hut and walked toward the upper riverbank. Suddenly, he hurried forward and stooped
over an Indian lying face down on the bank. A
trickle of blood was coming from what was the
beginning of a massive bruise on the base of his
neck. His fellow tribesman straightened and began
to shout, repeatedly and urgently.

Hamilton momentarily ceased paddling and
glanced involuntarily over his shoulder. Then he

bent himself again to his task but with even more energy this time.

Ramon and Navarro, as by prearrangement, had already begun to move to the other end of the island. Now they stopped abruptly when they heard the cry ashore, a cry now taken up by the shouting of many more angry voices.

Ramon said, "I think Señor Hamilton has been up to something. I also think we'd better wait a little."

The two men crouched on the island shore, rifles at the ready, and peered out across the channel. The bulky outline of Hamilton's launch and the two canoes he was towing were now visible not thirty yards from where they were. Not as visible, but still distinct enough to be unmistakable, were the shadowy forms of canoes putting out from the village in pursuit.

Ramon shouted, "As close to the island as you can. We'll cover you."

Hamilton glanced over his shoulder. The nearest of half a dozen canoes was already less than thirty yards away. Two men stood in the bows, one with a blowpipe to his mouth, the other pulling back the string of his bow.

Hamilton crouched as low as possible in the boat, glancing almost desperately to his right. He could now see both Ramon and Navarro, and he could see that they had their rifles leveled. The two shots came simultaneously. The warrior with the blowpipe toppled backward in the canoe; the one with the drawn bow pitched into the water, his arrow hissing harmlessly into the river.

"Quickly," Hamilton called. "Get to the others."

Ramon and Navarro loosed a few shots, more for the sake of discouragement than with the intent of hitting anything, then began to run. Thirty seconds later they joined the remainder of the party at the downstream end of the island, all looking anxiously upriver. Hamilton was struggling, unsuccessfully, to bring his unwieldly trio of boats ashore: It looked as if he would miss the tip of the island by feet only.

Ramon and Navarro handed over their rifles, plunged into the river, seized the bows of the motor launch, and turned it into the shore. There were no orders given, no shouts for haste: Such were needless. Within seconds all the equipment and passengers were aboard the launch, the boat pushed off, and paddles distributed. They cast frequent and apprehensive glances astern, but there was no cause for concern. The canoes, unmistakably, were dropping behind. There was going to be no pursuit.

Smith said, not even grudgingly, "That was well managed, Hamilton. And now?"

"First we bail. There should be three cooking pans floating around somewhere. Then we move out into the middle of the river—just in case they've sent some sharpshooters down the left bank. There's going to be a full moon shortly, the skies are cloudless, so we might as well carry on. Kellner and Hiller must be distinctly worried about us by this time."

Tracy said, "Why the two empty canoes?"

"I said yesterday that there were falls about fifty miles below the town. That's why we had to airlift the hovercraft beyond them. The falls are about twenty miles farther on. We'll have to make a portage there, and it would be impossible to make it with this elephant. When we get there and have emptied her, we'll give her a shove over the edge. Maybe she'll survive, the falls are only fifteen feet."

Some little time later the now bailed out motor launch glided gently down the center of the river, six men at the paddles but not exerting themselves; the current bore them along. The newly risen moon gleamed softly on the brown water. It was a peaceful scene.

Five hours later, as Hamilton guided the launch into the left bank, the passengers could distinctly hear the sound of the falls ahead, no Niagara roar, but unmistakably falls. They made the bank and tied up to a tree. The portage was not more than a hundred yards. First, all the equipment, food, and personal luggage was carried down, then the two canoes, and just in case the motor launch should survive its fall, the three cooking utensils for bailing as well.

Hamilton and Navarro climbed into a canoe and reached a spot where the white water ended about a hundred feet below the foot of the falls and paddled gently to maintain position. Both men were

looking upriver toward the falls beyond which, the
knew, Ramon was at work.

For half a minute there was only the brown
white smoothness of the Rio da Morte sliding ver
tically downward. Then the bows of the moto
launch came in sight, appeared to hesitate, unt
suddenly the entire boat was over and plunging
down. There was a loud smack and a considerabl
cloud of spray. The launch first entered the water
then disappeared entirely. All of ten seconds elapse
before it reappeared. But reappear it did, and, re
markably, right side up.

The launch, so full of water that there were onl
about four inches of freeboard left, drifted sluggishl
downstream until Hamilton got a line aboard. Wit
no little difficulty he and Navarro towed it to th
left bank and tied up. New bailing operations com
menced.

The brightly illuminated hovercraft lay anchore
in midriver. Navigation, deck, and cabin lights wer
on. Kellner and Hiller were close to despair becaus
the expected arrivals were already fifteen hours late
and it hardly seemed likely that if they hadn't ar
rived by that time, they would be arriving at all
They had no cause for concern as far as they them
selves were concerned. They had only to continu
downriver till they came to the junction with th
Araguaia and some form of civilization. Both mei
were prepared to wait indefinitely and both for th
same unexplained reason, which neither would ad

t: They had faith in Hamilton's powers of sur-
val. And so Kellner had his hovercraft lit up like
Christmas tree. He was taking no chances that the
licopter would bypass him in the darkness.

He and Hiller, both men with their machine pis-
ls immediately and constantly ready to hand, stood
 the brief afterdeck between the fans, ears always
aining for the first faint intimation of the rackety
mor of the Sikorsky. But it was his eyes that gave
ellner the answer he was waiting for, not his ears.
e peered upriver, peered more closely, then
itched on and trained the hovercraft's powerful
archlight.

A powerless and impassively manned motor
unch and two canoes had just appeared in line
ead round a bend in the Rio da Morte.

EIGHT

THE HOVERCRAFT'S CABIN WAS luxuriously furnished although on a necessarily small scale. The bar was splendidly if selectively equipped and, at the moment, well patronized. Most of the passengers from the wrecked helicopter having escaped death, the atmosphere was relaxed, almost convivial, and the spirit of the departed Heffner did not appear to hover over the company.

Hamilton said to Kellner, "Any trouble during the night?"

"Not really. A couple of canoe-loads of Indians approached us just after midnight. We turned the searchlight on them and they turned and headed back for shore."

"No shooting?"

"None."

"Good. Now, the big question tomorrow is the rapids that the Indians call the Hoehna."

"Rapids?" Kellner said. "There are no rapids shown on the chart."

"Yeah. Nevertheless, they're there. Never been through them myself, although I've seen them from the air. Don't look anything special from up there, but then nothing ever does. Much experience with rapids?"

"A bit," Kellner said. "Nothing that a boat hasn't navigated through."

"I'm told boats have made it through the Hoehna."

"So where's the problem? A hovercraft can navigate rapids that no boat made by man could ever hope to."

Serrano said, "Knowing you, Señor Hamilton, I thought you would have had us on our way by this time. A clear night. Bright moon. A beautiful night for sailing. Or is it 'flying' in one of those machines?"

"We need a good night's rest, all of us. It's going to be a hard day tomorrow. The Hoehna rapids are less than a hundred miles away. How long to get there, Kellner?"

"Three hours. Less, if you want."

"No. You don't navigate rapids by night. And only a madman goes there in the hours of darkness."

"What next?" Smith said.

"The Horena," Hamilton replied.

Tracy said, "The Horena? Another Indian tribe?"

"Yes."

"Like the Chapate?"

"They're not at all like the Chapate. The Horena

are the Roman lions, the Chapate the Christians. The Horena put the fear of living death into the Chapate."

"But you said the Muscias—"

"Ah! The Muscias are to the Horena what the Horena are to the Chapate. Or so they say. Good night."

"Rapids!" Ramon called out. "Rapids ahead!"

In the two and a half hours since the hovercraft's dawn departure, the Rio da Morte, though flowing at a rate of about fifteen knots, had been almost glassily calm, and although visibility had been poor because of fairly heavy rain, no problems had been encountered. Now conditions had dramatically altered. At first indistinctly through the now sheeting rain, but then suddenly, frighteningly, and all too vividly rocks could be seen, some jagged, some curved, thrusting up from the riverbed. For as far as the eye could see hundreds of them spanned the entire width of the river with white-veined, seething water coursing down between them. The hovercraft, throttled back to a point where directional control could just be maintained, was almost at once into this white and seething cauldron.

When Kellner had said that he had some little experience of navigating rapids, he had been doing himself less than justice. As far as the untrained observer could see, he was masterly. He was positively dancing a jig at the controls. He no longer had the throttle pulled back but kept altering it between half and full ahead which, considering their speed, might have seemed foolhardy, but wasn't. By doing this and by ignoring the air ducts and maintaining the cushion pressure as high as possible, he could all the more easily avoid making violent course alterations which would have slued the hovercraft broadside and into disaster. Instead, he was deliberately aiming for and riding his hovercraft over the less fearsome rocks in his path.

Even here he had to be selective, searching out the more rounded rocks and avoiding the jagged ones which, at that speed, would have ripped even the abnormally tough apron skirts, leading to the collapse of the cushion and turning the hovercraft into a boat, which would then have foundered in short order. One moment he was jerking the pitch control back, putting power on the left fan, then if this proved insufficient, applying right rudder to give him directional stability while only seconds later he had to reverse the procedure. His task was made harder by the fact that even the high-speed windshield wipers were capable only intermittently of clearing the spray and rain.

Kellner said to Hamilton, who was seated beside him, "Tell me again about all those boats that were supposed to navigate the Hoehna."

"Guess I must have been misinformed."

Farther back in the hovercraft no one spoke because all their energies were concentrated on hanging on to their seats. The general effect of the motion was that of a roller coaster—except that this roller coaster, unlike the fairground type, also shook violently from side to side.

Up front, Kellner said, "Do you see what I see?"

Some fifty yards ahead the river appeared to come to an abrupt end. They were approaching a waterfall of sorts.

"Unfortunately. What are you going to do about it?"

"Funny."

The hovercraft was being swept helplessly along. The drop in the river level must have been at least ten feet. Kellner was doing the only thing he could do—trying to keep the hovercraft on a perfectly straight course.

The hovercraft swept over the fall, dipped sharply, and plunged downward at an angle of forty-five degrees. With an explosion of sound and spray, the hovercraft momentarily disappeared save for the stern. Not only the bows but part of the front of the cabin went completely under and in that way and at that angle the hovercraft remained for several seconds before it slowly struggled to the surface again, water cascading off its decks. It settled deeper in the water, the effect of partially losing its air cushion when the stern had come completely clear of the water.

The interior of the craft was a scene of appalling confusion. The angle of fall and the stunning impact had catapulted everyone to the deck. Equipment that had been stored but not lashed aft was now scattered throughout the cabin. To make matters worse, a window had been smashed and hundreds of gallons of water were sloshing about the interior of the cabin. One by one the passengers struggled upright. They were bruised, dazed, and slightly concussed, but there seemed to be no broken bones.

As the air cushion began to fill again and the water gurgled away through the self-draining ports, they could feel the hovercraft rise slowly to its normal position.

Three times in the next few minutes the hovercraft went through a similar experience, although none of the overfalls were as high as the first time. At last the hovercraft passed into an area of smooth, rock-free water, and it was then that another danger manifested itself. The forested banks gave way to what was at first low rock, which quickly became higher and higher until they were passing through what was virtually a cliff-sided canyon. At the same time the river swiftly narrowed to about a third of its original width, and the speed of the river—and hence that of the hovercraft—rapidly more than doubled.

Hamilton and Kellner stared through the windshield, glanced at each other, then looked forward again. Ahead, the steep-sided river walls fell sharply away, but this was no help. A quarter of a mile ahead a jumble of huge black rocks blocked the river from side to side.

"Bloody charts!" Kellner said.

"Indeed."

"Pity, really. These machines are very expensive."

"Make for the left."

"Any particular reason?"

"The Horena live on the right bank."

"Left, as the man says."

The rocks were about three hundred yards away. They appeared to form an impenetrable barrier, no two sufficiently far apart to afford passage for the hovercraft.

Hamilton and Kellner looked at each other. Simultaneously they shrugged. Hamilton turned and faced the rear.

"Hang on tight," he said. "We're about to stop very suddenly." He had no sooner spoken than he realized that his warning had been unnecessary. They had seen what was coming up. They were already hanging on for dear life.

The rocks were now no more than a hundred yards distant. Kellner was guiding the craft toward the biggest gap between any two of them, the first and the second from the left bank.

For a moment it seemed that the hovercraft might just make the passage as Kellner arrowed straight for the center of the gap. The craft's bows passed through but that was all: The passage was at least eighteen inches narrower than the midships beam of the hovercraft. With a grinding, screeching tearing of metal, the hovercraft came to an abrupt halt, immovably jammed.

Kellner went into reverse and applied maximum power. Nothing happened. Kellner eased off the fans but kept the engine running to maintain the cushion. He straightened up, muttering to himself, "Now with an ocean-going tug . . ."

Ten minutes later there was a pile of rucksacks, canvas bags, and other improvised luggage containers on deck and Hamilton was securing a rope around his waist. He said, "It's only twenty feet to that bank, but the water's mighty fast so kindly don't let go of the end of that rope."

It was a danger, but not the only one. Even as he finished speaking there came a sudden grunt and Kellner collapsed to the deck. A dart protruded from the back of his neck. Hamilton swung round.

On the far right bank, less than fifty yards away, stood a group of Indians, ten or twelve in all. Every man had a blowpipe to his mouth.

"Horena!" Hamilton shouted. "Down! Take cover behind the cabin, inside the cabin. Ramon! Navarro!"

Almost immediately, Ramon and Navarro, all humanitarian principles forgotten at the sight of Kellner, were on the cabin roof, stretched out on their elbows, rifles in hand. More darts struck the metal sheathing but none found a target. In seconds the twins fired six shots. At five hundred yards both men were accurate. At fifty yards they were deadly. One after another, in those few seconds, three Horena toppled into the river, three others crumpled and died where they stood, and the others melted away.

Hamilton gazed down in bitterness at the lifeless

Kellner. Not for the Horena the use of timbo, the poisonous bark of a forest vine which simply stunned: The dart which took Kellner had been tipped with curare.

Hamilton said, "Damn! If it weren't for Kellner we'd all be dead. And now Kellner is dead." Without another word he jumped into the river. The only danger here, he knew, was the speed of the water: Neither alligators nor piranha inhabit rapids.

At first he was swept downstream and had to be hauled back. In the second attempt he succeeded in reaching the bank. He stood there some time, regaining his breath—the buffeting had been severe—then undid the rope around his waist and secured it to the bole of a tree. Another rope was thrown across to him. This he passed round a branch and threw the free end back to the hovercraft, where, in turn, it was passed round a fan bracket and thrown back to Hamilton, forming, in effect, an endless pulley.

The first item of equipment—Hamilton's own rucksack—was ferried across, well clear of the water, as was all the rest of the equipment. The members of the party had to make it the wet way.

NINE

Sweat-soaked and stumbling, mostly from near exhaustion, the heavily laden party of nine made their painfully slow way through the afternoon gloom of the rain forest. Even at high noon there was never more than half-light in its depths. The crowns of the great liana-festooned trees stretched out and intertwined a hundred feet or more above the ground, effectively blocking out the sunlight.

Progress was slow not because they had to hack their way with machetes through the dense undergrowth, because of dense undergrowth there was none. For plants to grow at ground level, sunshine is essential. Jungle, in the true African sense of the term, did not exist. The progress was slow primarily because there was as much swampland as there was firm ground, and quicksands were an ever-present peril. A man could step confidently onto what appeared to be an inviting stretch of greensward and on his second step find himself shoulder deep in a swamp. For safe locomotion in the forest, a probe, in the form of a hacked-off and trimmed branch, was essential. For every mile covered as the crow flew, it was not uncommon to have to traverse five miles. That, and the time it took to locate patches of firm ground, made for time-consuming, frustrating, exhausting travel.

Smith, in particular, was finding the going rough. His clothes were so saturated with sweat that he might well have just been dragged from the river minutes before. His legs had gone rubbery, and he was gasping for breath.

Smith said, "What the hell are you trying to prove, Hamilton? How tough you are and how out of condition we are? God's sake man, a break. An hour wouldn't kill us, would it?"

"No. But the Horena might."

"You said their territory was on the right bank."

"That's what I believe. But don't forget, we killed six of their men. Great lads for revenge, the Horena. I wouldn't put it past them to have crossed the river and be following us. There could be a hundred of them within a hundred yards of here, just waiting to get within blowpipe range, and we wouldn't know a thing about it until too late."

Smith, it appeared, was possessed of reserves of strength and endurance of which he had been unaware. He hurried on.

* * *

Toward evening, they reached a small, swampy earing. Most of the party were now shambling, not alking.

"Enough," Hamilton said. "We'll make camp."

With the approach of dusk the forest appeared come alive. All around them was sound. Mainly, came from birds—parrots, macaws, parakeets. ut there was animal life too. Monkeys screeched, ullfrogs barked, and now and again the deeply uffled roar of a jaguar came at them from the epth of the forest.

Everywhere there were creepers, vines, parasitic rchids, and there in the clearing exotic flowers of most every conceivable color. The air was damp nd fetid, a miasmic smell all-prevalent, the heat verpowering and leaden and enervating, the floor nderfoot almost an unbroken expanse of thick, inging, evil-smelling mud.

Everyone, even Hamilton, sank gratefully to hat few patches of dry ground they could find. ver the river, not much higher than the treetops, everal birds, with huge wingspreads, seemed suspended against the sky, for their wings were motionss. They looked evil, sinister.

Maria said, "What are those horrible-looking reatures?"

"Urubus," Hamilton said. "Amazonian vultures. hey seem to be looking for something."

Maria shuddered. Everybody gazed unhappily at e vultures.

"A poor choice, I suppose," Hamilton said. "The

cooking pots, headhunters, or the vultures. A▮
speaking of cooking pots, some fresh meat mig▮
help. Curassow—a kind of wild turkey—armadill▮
wild boar, all very tasty. Navarro?"

Ramon said, "I'll come too."

"You stay, Ramon. A little more thoughtfulnes▮
please. Someone has to look after those poor souls▮

Tracy said, "To keep an eye on us, you mean."

"I don't see what mischief you can get up to here▮

"Your haversack."

"I don't understand."

Tracy said deliberately, "Heffner appeared ▮
find something there just before you murder▮
him."

Ramon said, "Before Mr. Heffner met his u▮
fortunate end is what Mr. Tracy means."

Hamilton eyed Tracy thoughtfully, then turne▮
away into the forest, Navarro following. Less th▮
two hundred yards from the camp Hamilton put ▮
restraining hand on Navarro's arm and pointe▮
ahead. Not forty yards away was a *quiexada*. Th▮
most savage of all the world's wild boars is ▮
devoid of fear that it has been known to inva▮
towns in herds, driving the citizens into their house▮

"Supper," Hamilton said.

Navarro nodded and raised his rifle. One sh▮
was all that Navarro would need. He fired and th▮
began to make their way toward the dead anim▮
Then they halted abruptly. A herd of perhaps thr▮
dozen *quiexada* had suddenly appeared from t▮
forest. They halted, pawed the ground, and cam▮
on again. There was no mistaking their intention.

Only on the riversides do Amazonian trees have ordinary branches, for only there can they get sunlight. Hamilton and Navarro reached the lowermost branches of the nearest tree a short distance ahead of the boars, which proceeded to encircle the tree. Navarro said something to the effect of thank God, they could breathe easy, but Hamilton said, "Don't."

As if in response to some unseen signal, the boars began to use their vicious tusks to savage the roots of the trees. The roots of the Amazonian trees, like those of the giant sequoia of California, are extremely long—and extremely shallow.

"I would say they have done this sort of thing before, Señor," Navarro said. "How long is this going to take, do you think?"

"Not long at all."

Hamilton sighted his pistol and shot a *quiexada* that seemed to be more industrious than its companions. The dead animal toppled into the river. Within seconds, the smooth surface of the river was disturbed by a myriad ripples, and there came the high-pitched, spine-chilling buzzing whine as the needle teeth of the voracious piranha proceeded to strip the *quiexada* to the bone.

Navarro cleared his throat. "Perhaps," he said, "you should have shot one not quite so close to the river."

Hamilton said, "*Quiexada* to one side, piranha to the other. You don't by any chance see a constrictor lurking in the branches above?"

Involuntarily, Navarro glanced upward, then down at the boars which had redoubled their efforts.

Both men started firing and within seconds a dozen *quiexada* lay dead.

Navarro said, "Next time I go boar hunting—if there is a next time—I'll bring a submachine gun with me. My magazine is empty."

"Mine too."

The sight of their dead companions seemed only to increase the blood lust of the boars. They tore at the roots with savage frenzy—and, already, several of the roots had been severed.

Navarro said, "Señor Hamilton, either I'm shaking or this tree is becoming rather—what is the word for it?"

"Wobbly?"

"Wobbly."

"I don't think. I know."

A rifle shot rang out and a boar dropped dead. Hamilton and Navarro swung round to look back the way they had come. Ramon, who seemed to be carrying a pack of some sort on his back, was less than forty yards away and was prudently standing by a low-branched tree. He fired steadily and with deadly accuracy. Suddenly an empty click was heard. Hamilton and Navarro looked at each other thoughtfully, but Ramon remained unperturbed. He reached into his pocket, extracted another magazine clip, fitted it, and resumed firing. Three more shots and it finally dawned on the *quiexada* that they were in a no-win contest. Those that remained turned and ran off into the forest.

The three men walked back toward the camp,

dragging a *quiexada* behind them. Ramon said, "I heard the shooting so I came. Of course, I brought plenty of spare ammunition with me." Deadpan, he patted a bulging pocket, then shrugged apologetically. "All my fault. I should never have let you go alone. One has to be a man of the forest—"

"Oh, shut up," Hamilton said. "Thoughtful of you to bring my rucksack along with you."

Ramon said pontifically, "One should not expose the weak-minded to temptation."

"Do be quiet," Navarro said. He turned to Hamilton. "God only knows he was insufferable enough before. But now, after this—"

The cooking fire burned in the near darkness and boar steaks sizzled in a glowing bed of coals.

Smith said, "I appreciate the necessity for all the shooting. But if the Horena are around—well, those shots must have attracted the attention of everyone within miles."

"No worry," Hamilton said. "No Horena will ever attack at night. If he dies at night his soul will wander forever in the hereafter. His gods must see him die."

He prodded a steak with his sheath knife. "I would say those are just about ready." Ready or not the steaks were dispatched with gusto, and when they were finished Hamilton said, "Better if it had hung a week, but tasty, tasty. Okay, bed. We leave at dawn. I'll keep the first watch."

They prepared for sleep, some lying on waterproof sheets, others in lightweight hammocks slung between trees at the edge of the clearing. Hamilton flung some fuel on the fire and kept on flinging it until it flared up so brightly that the flames were almost ten feet high. Machete in hand, Hamilton departed to obtain some more fuel and returned with an armful of branches most of which he cast on the already blazing fire.

Smith said, "Well, granted, you know how to make bonfires. But what's it all for? You cold?"

"Safety measure. Keeps the creepy-crawlies at bay. Wild animals fear fire."

He was to be proved half right, half wrong.

Hamilton was on his third fuel-hunting trip and was returning to camp when he heard the piercing scream of fear. He dropped the fuel and ran into the brightly lit clearing. He knew the high-pitched scream could only have come from Maria and as he closed on her hammock the reason for her terror was obvious: An anaconda, at least thirty feet in length and with its tail still anchored to one of the trees that supported Maria's hammock, had one of its deadly coils wrapped round the base of her hammock. She was in no way pinned down, just too paralyzed with fear to move. The anaconda's vast jaws were agape.

It was not Hamilton's first anaconda and he had a nodding respect for them, but no more. A full-grown specimen can swallow a 150-pound prey in its entirety. But while they could be endlessly patient, even cunning, in waiting for their next meal

happen along, they were extremely slow-witted
action. While Maria continued to scream in
rror, he approached within feet of the fearsome
ad. No more than any other creature on earth
uld an anaconda withstand three Luger bullets
the head: It died immediately, but even in its
ath the coil slipped over the girl's ankles and
ntinued to contract. Hamilton struggled to pull the
my coil free but was brushed aside by Ramon,
ho carefully placed two rifle bullets into the upper
nter of the coil, severing the main spinal nerve.
he anaconda at once went limp.

Hamilton carried Maria across to his ground-
eet close by the fire. She was in a state of mild
ock. Keep a shocked patient warm, Hamilton had
ten heard, and the thought had no sooner occurred
him than Ramon knelt alongside, a sleeping bag
his hands. Together they eased the girl inside,
pped up the bag, and sat to wait. Navarro came to
in them and jerked a thumb in the direction of
nith, curled up in a sleeping position.

"Observe our gallant hero," he said. "Asleep?
e's wide awake. Has been all the time. I watched
m."

Ramon said, complaining, "You might have come
d watched us."

"When you and Señor Hamilton can't take care
f a simple-minded reptile like that, it's time for us
l to give up. I saw his face and he was terrified,
emed quite unable to move—not, I am sure, that
e wanted to move or had any intention of moving.
as the girl been hurt?"

"Not physically," Hamilton said. "I'm afraid th is basically my fault. I had a big fire going to fright off wild animals. Well, anacondas are wild and frightened of fire as any other. This one just want out. It was the devil's bad luck that it was roostin in the tree that helped support Maria's hammoc I'm pretty sure she would have come to no harm. T reptile was simply easing its way down the tre Apart from the fact that its belly is swollen an obviously would not be requiring another meal f a fortnight, it probably had a much greater matt on its mind, such as getting the hell out of here. A very unfortunate, but no harm done."

"Perhaps," Ramon said. "I hope."

"You hope?" Hamilton said.

"Trauma," Ramon said. "How deep does a traum go? This has been a traumatic experience." H paused, dug a finger into a tooth. "But I think tha only a side issue. I have the feeling that her who life has been a traumatic experience."

"You plunging into the deep waters of psycho ogy, Ramon?" Hamilton didn't smile as he spok

"I agree with Ramon," Navarro said. "Twin you know," he added apologetically. "Something wrong—or not what it appears to be. Her action her behavior, the way she talks and smiles . . . I fi it hard to believe that this is a bad person, a con mon whore. Or an expensive one. Smith, we kno is a bad person. She doesn't care for him; any fo can see that. So what goes?"

"Well," Hamilton said judicially, "he's got a l to offer—"

"Ignore the señor," Ramon said. "He's just try-
ıg to provoke us."

Navarro nodded in agreement, then said, "I think
ıe is a prisoner in some way or another."

"Possibly," Hamilton said. "Possibly. Has it oc-
urred to either of you that *he* might be in some way
er prisoner, without knowing it?"

Navarro looked at Ramon, and accusingly at
[amilton. "There you go again, Señor. You know
ɔmething that we don't know, and you're not tell-
ıg us."

"I know almost nothing that you don't know.
ar be it from me to suggest that at times I look
ıore closely and, perhaps, think a little more
eeply. But, then, you are young."

"Young?" Navarro was indignant. "Neither of
s, Señor Hamilton, will ever see thirty again."

"That's what I meant."

He put his fingers to his lips. Beside him, Maria
ʼas stirring. She opened her eyes, still huge with
orror. Hamilton touched her gently on the shoul-
er.

"It's all right now," he said softly. "It's all over."

"That horrible ghastly head." Her voice was no
ıore than a husky whisper and she was shaking.
.amon rose and walked away. "That awful snake—"

"The snake is dead," Hamilton said. "And you
re unharmed. We promise, no harm will come ʈo
ou."

She lay there breathing shallowly, her eyes closed.
he opened them again when Ramon returned and

knelt by her side. He had an aluminum cup in on hand, a bottle in the other.

Hamilton said, "And what do we have here?"

"The finest cognac," Ramon replied. "As ex pected. Smith's private supply."

"I don't like brandy," she said.

"Ramon is right. You'd better like it. You nee it."

Ramon poured a generous measure. She taste it, coughed, screwed her eyes shut, and emptied th cup in two gulps.

"Good girl," Hamilton said.

"Awful," she said. She looked at Ramon. "B thank you. I feel better already." She glanced acros the clearing and fear touched her eyes again. "Th hammock—"

"You're not going back to that hammock," Ham ilton said. "It's safe enough now, of course, it wa just sheer bad luck that the anaconda was up th tree when your hammock was slung, but we ca understand your not wanting to go back there You're in Ramon's sleeping bag and on a ground sheet. You'll stay just where you are. We'll keep big fire going all night, and one of the three of u will keep an eye on you till the morning. I promise Not even a mosquito will come near you."

Slowly she looked at the three men in turn, the said huskily, "You are all very kind to me." Sh tried to smile, but it was only a try. "Damsel i distress. Is that it?"

"Perhaps there's a little bit more to it than that

Iamilton said. "But now's not the time to talk about
. Just you try to sleep—I'm sure Ramon will give
ou a nightcap to help you on your way. Oh, hell."

Smith, who obviously felt that he had maintained
is distance long enough, was approaching, his
vhole attitude manifesting his resentment of Maria's
lose proximity to the three men. As he dropped to
is knees beside her, Hamilton rose, looked at him,
urned, and walked away, the twins following.

Ramon said, "Señor Hamilton, we said we would
ollow you anywhere, and we have. *Quiexada*, pi-
anha, anaconda, a sick girl, and a complaining
villain. To pick so divine a resting spot in such
unique company is a gift not given to many."

Hamilton just looked at him and moved off into
he forest to retrieve his load of firewood.

Early in the morning Hamilton led the others in
single file through the rain forest and across firm
ground, firm because the terrain was gently rising
and the water table was now well below them. After
about two hours' walking, Hamilton stopped and
waited until the others gathered round him.

"From here on," Hamilton said, "no talking. Not
one word. And watch where you put your feet. I
don't want to hear as much as the crackle of a
broken twig. Understood?" He looked at Maria,
who looked pale and exhausted, not so much from
the rigors of the walk, for there had been none, but
because she had not slept at all: The previous night's
experience, as Ramon had said, had been something

more than traumatic. "It's not much farther. Ha
an hour, at most, then we'll have a rest and carr
on during the afternoon."

"I'm all right," she said. "It's just that I'm begin
ning to hate this rain forest. I suppose you'll b
telling me again that no one asked me to come."

"A snake on every tree, is that it?"

She nodded.

"No more worry," Hamilton said. "You'll neve
again spend a night in this forest. That's anothe
promise."

Tracy said slowly, "I take it that that can mea
only one thing. We'll be in the Lost City tonight.

"If things go as I hope, yes."

"You know where you are."

"Yes."

"You've known ever since we left the hovercraft.'

"True. How did you know?"

"Because you haven't used your compass since.'

Half an hour later, exactly as he had forecast
Hamilton, finger to his lips, stopped and waited fo
the others to come up to him. When he spoke, it wa
in a whisper.

"On your lives. Not a sound. Stay hidden until
tell you otherwise. On your hands and knees, the
lie prone until I give the word."

And so on hands and knees they advanced i
silence. Hamilton dropped forward and eased him
self slowly ahead, using elbows and toes. He stoppe
again and waited until the others had joined him
He pointed forward, through the trees.

In a lush green valley below them they could see an Indian village. There were dozens of large huts and, in the center, a communal hut, which looked as if it could accommodate at least two hundred people with ease. The place seemed to be deserted until suddenly a small copper-colored child appeared carrying a flint ax and a nut which he placed on a flat stone and proceeded to belabor. It was like a scene from the Stone Age, from the dawn of prehistory. A laughing woman, statuesque and also copper-colored, emerged from the same hut and picked up the child.

In slow wonderment, Tracy said, "That color? That appearance? Those aren't Indians."

"Keep your voice down," Hamilton said urgently. "They're Indians all right, but they do not come from the Amazon basin. They come from the Pacific."

Tracy stared at him, still in wonderment, and shook his head.

Suddenly people, scores of them, began to emerge from the communal hut. That they were not Amazonian Indians was underscored by the fact that there were as many women as men among them: Normally, in the Amazonian basin, women are banned from the meeting places of elders and warriors. All were of the same copper color, all possessed of a proud, almost regal bearing. They began to disperse toward their huts.

Smith touched Hamilton on the arm and said in a low voice, "Who are those people?"

"The Muscias."

Smith turned pale. "Goddamned Muscias!" he said in a vicious whisper. "What the hell are you playing at? Headhunters, you said. Headshrinkers! Cannibals! I'm off!"

"Off to where, you clown? You've got no place left to run to. Stay here. *Don't, don't, don't* show yourselves."

The advice was superfluous. No one had the slightest intention of showing himself.

Hamilton rose and walked confidently into the clearing. He had gone at least ten paces before he was noticed. There was a sudden silence, the babble of voices ceased; then the chatter redoubled in volume. An exceptionally tall Indian, old and with his forearms almost covered in gold bracelets, gazed for some seconds, then ran forward. He and Hamilton embraced.

The old man, who it soon became apparent was the chief, and Hamilton engaged in an animated, incomprehensible conversation. The chief, with an expression of incredulity on his face, repeatedly shook his head. Just as firmly Hamilton nodded his. Suddenly, Hamilton extended his right arm and made a semicircular motion, bringing his arm to a sudden stop. The chief looked long at him, seized him by the arms, smiled, and nodded his head. He turned and spoke rapidly to his people.

Tracy said, "I'd say those two have met somewhere before."

The chief finished addressing his people, all of whom had now gathered in the clearing, and spoke again to Hamilton, who nodded and turned.

Hamilton shouted to his waiting companions, You can come now. Keep your hands well away om any weapon."

Not quite dazedly, but not understanding what as happening, the other eight members of the party ntered the clearing.

Hamilton said, "This is Chief Corumba." He itroduced each of the eight in turn. The chief ravely acknowledged each introduction, shaking ach in turn by hand.

Hiller muttered, "But Indians don't shake hands."

Maria touched Hamilton on the arm. "But those avage headhunters—"

"These are the kindliest, most gentle, most peaceble people on earth. In their language they do not ave a word for war because they do not know what ar is. They are a lost children from a lost age— nd the people who built the Lost City."

"And I thought I knew more about the Mato Grosso tribes than any man alive," Serrano said.

"And so you may, Serrano. If, that is to say, I can ake the word of Colonel Diaz."

"Colonel Diaz?" Smith said. He was floundering n deep water. "Who's Colonel Diaz?"

"A friend of mine."

Tracy said, "But their ferocious reputation—"

"A fiction invented by Dr. Hannibal Huston."

"Who the hell is Hannibal Huston?"

"The man who found these lost people. He hought that such a reputation might ensure them— vhat shall we say?—a little privacy."

"Huston?" Hiller said. "Huston? You—you foun Huston?"

"Years ago."

"But you've only been in the Mato Grosso fo four months."

"This time. I've known it for many years. Re member in the Hotel de Paris in Romono you talke about my search for the golden people. I forgot t mention that I met them years ago. Here they are The Children of the Sun."

Maria said, "And Dr. Huston is still in the Los City?"

"He's still there, I believe. Come, I think thes good people want to offer us some hospitality. First however, I owe you a small explanation abou them."

"High time, too," Smith said. "Why all the dra matic, stealthy approach to them?"

"Because if we had approached noisily, as group, they would have run away. They have ever good reason to fear those from the outside world We are, ironically, known as the *civilizados*. I practically everything that matters they're a damne sight more civilized than we are. We bring then so-called progress, which harms them; so-calle change, which harms them; so-called civilization which harms them even more; and disease, whicl kills them. These people have no natural resistanc to measles or influenza. Either of those are to then what bubonic plague was to Europeans and Asiatic in the Middle Ages. Half a tribe can be wiped ou in a fortnight. The same thing happened to th

eople of Tierra del Fuego. Well-meaning mission-
ries gave them simple clothes, primarily so that
he women could cover their nakedness. The blan-
ets came from a hospital where there had been a
measles epidemic. Most of the people were wiped
ut."

Tracy said, "But our presence here. That must
ndanger them?"

"No. Almost half the Muscias were destroyed by
measles or influenza or a combination of both. These
eople here are the survivors. They acquired nat-
ral immunity the hard way."

The group was momentarily silent, the Indians
ooking at Hamilton's tribe, the oddly assorted Ham-
ton party trying to see behind the splendid Indian
aces into minds masked by language.

"As I said, it was Dr. Huston who found them.
Although mainly famous as an explorer, his real
fe's work was something else. He was one of the
riginal *sertanistas*—men wise in jungle ways—and
founder member of the FUNAI, the National
oundation for the Indian, people who dedicate
heir lives to protecting the Indians and rendering
hem harmless to *civilizados*. 'Pacification' is the
erm generally used. In truth, what's mainly required
s protection *against* the *civilizados*. Sure, many of
he tribes were genuinely savage—well, not so many,
here are less than two hundred thousand pure-blood
ndians left—but their savagery came from fear, for
he most part, and which is understandable. Even
n modern times, those civilized gentlemen from the
uter world, and by no means all Brazilians, either,

have machine-gunned them, dynamited them from the air, and given them poisoned food."

"This is all news to me," Smith said, "and I've lived in this country for years. Frankly, I find it very hard to believe."

"Serrano will confirm it."

"I confirm it. You, too, are a *sertanista?*"

"Yes. Not always a very happy job. We have our failures. The Chapate and the Horena, as you've seen, are not too keen on the idea of cooperation with the outside world. And, inevitably, we still bring disease as we did here." He looked up, a musing tone gone from his voice. He was suddenly again all business.

"Come along, Chief Corumba is summoning us. We'll eat with them. It may taste a little odd, but smile. I can assure you that no harm will come to any of you."

One hour later the visitors were still seated around a rough wooden table outside the communal hut. Before them lay the remains of an excellent, exotic meal—game, fish, fruit, and unknown delicacies concerning the nature of which it had been thought more prudent not to ask. All had been washed down with *cachassa,* a potent brew. At the end, Hamilton rose, thanked Chief Corumba on behalf of all of them, and turned to the others.

"I think it's time we were on our way."

Tracy said, "One thing intrigues me. I've never *seen* so many gold ornaments in my life."

"Yeah, I thought that might intrigue you."

"Where do these people come from?"

"They don't know themselves. A lost people who have lost everything, and that includes their history. It was Dr. Huston's theory that they are the descendants of the Quimbaya, an ancient tribe from the Cauca or Magdalena valleys in the western Andes of Colombia."

Smith stared at him. "So what in God's name are they doing here?"

"Nobody knows. Huston thinks they left their homeland all those hundreds of years ago. He thinks they may have fled to the east, found the headwaters of the Amazon, come all the way down until they reached the Rio Tocantis, turned up that until they came to the Araguaia, then up the Rio da Morte. Again, who knows? Stranger migrations have happened. It could have taken them generations: They were said to be weighed down with possessions. I believe it. Wait till you see the Lost City, and you'll understand why I believe it."

Smith said, "How far away is this damned city?"

"Five hours. Six."

"Five hours!"

"And easy going. Uphill, but no swamps, no quicksands." He turned to Chief Corumba, who smiled and again warmly embraced Hamilton.

"Wishing us good luck?" Long John Silver said.

"Among quite a few other things. I'll have a longer chat with him tomorrow."

"Tomorrow!" Smith said.

"Why not?"

Smith, Tracy, and Hiller exchanged flickering glances. None of the three said anything.

Just before they walked away Hamilton spoke quietly to Maria. "Stay behind with these people. They will look after you, I promise. Where we're going is no place for a lady."

"I'm coming."

"Suit yourself." His tone turned cold. "There's an excellent chance you'll be dead by nightfall."

"You don't care much for me, do you?"

"Enough to ask you to stay behind."

In the late afternoon, Hamilton and his party were still making their way toward the Lost City. The going underfoot was excellent, dry, leafy, and springy.

Unfortunately, and especially for Smith, the incline was fairly severe and the heat was, as always, oppressive.

Hamilton said, "I think we'll have a half-hour break here. We're ahead of time—we can't move in until it's dark. Besides, some of you may think you've earned a rest."

"Too bloody right, we have," Smith said. "I was wondering how much longer you intended to crucify us?"

He sank wearily to the ground and mopped his streaming face with a bandana. He was not the only one to do so. With the exception of Hamilton, the twins, and Silver, everyone seemed to be suffering from a shortage of breath and leaden, aching legs. Hamilton had, indeed, been setting a brisk pace.

"You've done very well, all of you," Hamilton said. "Mind you, some of you might have done even better if you hadn't guzzled and drunk like pigs down in the village. We've climbed almost two thousand feet since leaving there."

Smith said, "How—much—longer?"

"From here to the top? Another half hour. No more. I'm afraid we'll have to do a bit more climbing after that—downhill, mind you, but a pretty steep downhill."

"Half an hour? Downhill?" Smith said. "Nothing."

"Wrong. Wait until you start going down."

"The last lap," Hamilton said. "We're ten yards from the brink of a ravine. Anyone who hasn't a head for heights had better say so now."

If anyone didn't have a head for heights, no one said so. Hamilton began to crawl forward. The rest followed. After a few minutes, Hamilton stopped. He lifted his head, lowered it, motioned to the others to move up beside him.

Hamilton said, "You see what I see?"

Smith said, "Jesus!"

Maria said, "The Lost City!"

Tracy said, "Shangri-la."

"El Dorado," Hamilton said.

"What?" Smith said. "What was that?"

"No, not really. There never was an El Dorado."

"Then why did you say it?"

"Just showing off. Amused. El Dorado means the golden man. New Inca rulers were covered in gold dust and dipped—only temporarily, of course—in a lake. You see that peculiar stepped pyramid with the flat top at the far end?"

The detail was unnecessary. Even in the gathering dusk, it was the dominant feature of the Lost City.

"That's one of the reasons—there are others—why Huston thought that the Children of the Sun came from Colombia. It's what you call a ziggurat. Originally it was a temple—tower in Babylonia or Assyria. No traces of those remain in the old world. The Egyptians built a different form of pyramid."

Tracy said, as if not knowing, "This is the only one?"

"By no means. You'll find well-preserved examples in Mexico, Guatemala, Bolivia, and Peru. But only in Central America and the northwest of South America. But nowhere else in the world—except here."

"So they're Andean," Serrano said. "You couldn't ask for better proof."

"You couldn't. But I have it."

"Complete proof? Total?"

"I'll show you later." He pointed with outstretched arm. "You see those steps?"

Stretching from the river to the top of the plateau and hewn from the vertical rock face, the stone tairway, awesome to look at even from a distance, ngled upward at forty-five degrees.

"Two hundred and forty eight steps," Hamilton aid, "each thirty inches wide. Worn, smooth, and lippery—and no handrail."

Tracy said, "Who counted them?"

"I did."

"You mean—"

"Yes. Wouldn't do it again, though. There had een a handrail once, and I'd brought along equip-nent to rig a rope rail. It's still on the hovercraft."

"Mr. Hamilton!" Long John Silver spoke in an rgent whisper. "Mr. Hamilton!"

"What's the excitement about?"

"Someone moving in the ruins down there."

"The pilot's eagle eye, eh? Good. We'll need your ight vision soon. There are a number of people own there. Why do you think I didn't fly in by elicopter?"

Serrano said, "They are not friends, no?"

"No." He turned to Smith. "Speaking of heli-opters, I don't have to explain the layout of this lace to you. You know it already."

"I don't understand."

"That film you had Hiller steal for you."

"I don't know what—"

"I took them a year ago. That's okay. I left no ption for Hiller but to steal the cassette. Taken rom a helicopter. Not bad for an amateur, were hey?"

Smith didn't say whether they were or not. He,

Hiller, and Tracy had again, momentarily, odd ex
pressions, mainly of deep unease.

Hamilton said, "Look to your left there—wher
the river forks to go round the island."

At a distance of about half a mile and abou
three hundred feet below their present elevation the
could just make out a spidery, sagging, and twistec
series of ropes, spanning the gorge between the top
of the plateau and a point about halfway up the top
of the cliff on which they were lying. Immediatel
below the cliffside anchorage a small waterfall arcec
out into the river.

"A rope bridge," Hamilton said. "Well, a lian.
bridge. Or a straw bridge. They're normally renewec
once a year. This one can't have been rebuilt for a
least five years. Must be in a pretty rotten state b
this time."

"So?" Smith said. The apprehension in his voic
was unmistakable.

"So that's the way we go in."

The silence that followed was long and profounc

At last Serrano said, "Another proof of Andea
ancestry. I mean, there *are* no rope bridges in th
Mato Grosso—well, there's not one now or, as fa
as I know, anywhere in Brazil. The Indians neve
learned how to make them. Why should they? The
never needed them. But the Incas and their descend
ants knew how to make them—in the Andes, the
had to know."

"I've seen one," Hamilton said. "On the Apurima
River, high up in Peru—about twelve thousan

feet. They use six heavy braided-straw cables for the main supports—four for the footpaths, two for the handrails. Smaller ropes for closing in the sides, and a bed of twigs spread over the footpath so that only a three-year-old could fall through. Can support scores of people when new."

"And this one?"

"I'm afraid this one is not new."

A narrow cleft ran down the cliff at an angle of close on sixty degrees. A small stream, fed from some spring above, fell, rather than flowed down this cleft, leaping whitely from spur to spur. On one side of this cleft a series of rough steps had been cut, a long time ago.

Hamilton and the others started to descend. It was an arduous descent but not as difficult or dangerous as it might have been; Hamilton had taken the precaution of binding together a series of tough lianas, anchoring one end to a tree and letting the rest fall down the cleft.

At the foot of the cleft, just above the point where the waterfall arced out above the river, a platform, about eight feet by eight, had been quarried out of the cliff face. Hamilton was already standing there. One by one he was joined by the others.

Hamilton moved to examine a stone bollard and an iron post that had been hammered into the platform. Three now threadbare lianas were attached to both. Hamilton produced his sheath knife and scraped at the iron post. Thick brown flakes were shaved away.

Two members of the party groaned.

"Keep your voices down," Hamilton said. "Rusty isn't it?" He turned away to look over the gorge. The others did the same. The straw bridge was flimsy and venerable and worse than it had appeared from above. Both the hand supports and the foot path were severely frayed. Several of the straw ropes had rotted and fallen away.

"Not exactly the George Washington or the Golden Gate. Well, what the hell. It's toll free."

Smith, his eyes wide, was appalled. "Good God! That's *suicide*. Only a madman would go on it. Do you expect me to risk my life on that?"

"Of course not. You wouldn't want to be certified as crazy. Why on earth should you risk your life? That's what you're paying me for. You're only here for the story, for the pictures. Tell you what. Give me your camera and I'll take the pictures for you. And don't forget—the people over there won't be welcoming trespassers."

Smith was silent for some time. Then he said, "I'm a man who sees things through to the end."

"Maybe the end is closer than you think. Swell. It's dark enough now. I'm going first."

Navarro said, "Señor Hamilton, I am much lighter—"

"Thank you. But that's just the point. I'm a heavy man and I'm carrying a heavy pack. If it takes my weight—well, you should all be okay."

"A thought occurs to me," Ramon said.

"And to me." He moved toward the straw bridge.

"What was that meant to mean?" Maria said.

"He thinks, perhaps, that they will have a man on the welcome mat out over there."

"Oh."

Hamilton moved slowly at first, then steadily across the straw bridge. That is, he made steady progress although not without problems. The bridge itself was shockingly unsteady, swaying from side to side. They peered after him, anxiously. When Hamilton was halfway across, the bridge sagged so badly in the middle that he had to haul himself up a steep incline. But he was experiencing little difficulty. He arrived safely on a platform similar to the one he had left on the other side of the gorge. There, he crouched low; the platform was only a few feet lower than the plateau. Cautiously, he lifted his head.

A guard was posted but was not taking his duties too seriously. Facing away from the gorge, he was smoking a cigarette and, of all things, relaxing in a deck chair. Hamilton's face registered disgust at guards who are never expecting visitors. In a second, Hamilton's bent arm was raised to shoulder level. His handkerchief-wrapped hand held the blade of his heavy sheath knife. The guard drew deeply on his cigarette, clearly illuminating his face. Hamilton made a small noise with his foot. The guard turned his head slightly. He made no sound as the haft of the knife struck him between the eyes; just tipped to one side and fell out of the chair.

Hamilton turned and flashed his torch three times. Within minutes he was joined one by one by eight people who were still shaking. They had not enjoyed their passage across the rope bridge.

Hamilton said, "Let's go and see the boss man." He could find his way blindfolded and led them silently past the fallen guard and through the ancient ruins. Shortly he stopped and pointed.

Ahead was a new wooden hall with lights showing. The sound of voices carried.

"Barracks," Hamilton said. "Mess hall and sleeping accommodation. Guards."

Tracy said, "Guards? Why that many? Who the hell else could get in here?"

"Guilty conscience somewhere."

"What's that noise?" Smith said.

"Generator."

"Where do we go from here?"

Hamilton pointed again. At the foot of the giant ziggurat was another but much smaller wooden building. Lights also shone from that building.

"There's where the guilty conscience lives." Hamilton was silent for a second. Then he added, "The man who every night feels dead feet trampling over his grave."

Silver said, "Hamilton—"

"Nothing, nothing. Ramon, Navarro. You see what I see?"

"Yes," Ramon said. "Two men standing in the shadow of that porch."

Hamilton seemed to ponder the situation. "I wonder what they could be doing there?"

"We'll go and ask them."

Ramon and Navarro melted into the shadows.

Smith said, "Who *are* these two? Your assistants, mean. They are not Brazilian."

"No."

"European?"

"Yes."

Ramon and Navarro returned as silently and unobtrusively as they had left.

"Well," Hamilton said. "What did they say?"

"Not a helluva lot," Navarro said. "They may ell us more when they wake up."

TEN

INSIDE THE SMALLER WOODEN house was a dining-cum-living room of substantial size. The walls were hung with flags, banners, portraits, swords, rapiers, guns, and pictures. Behind a table a large, red-faced, heavily jowled man was eating a solitary meal, washing it down with beer from a pewter liter mug beside him. He looked up, startled, as the door crashed open.

Hamilton, pistol in hand, was in the room. He was followed by Smith, then the others.

"Guten abend," Hamilton said. "I've brought an old friend along to see you."

He nodded toward Smith. "I think old friends should smile and shake hands and say 'Hello,' don't you? You don't?"

Hamilton's pistol fired, gouging a hole in the seated man's desk.

"Nervous hands," Hamilton said. "Ramon?"

Ramon went behind the desk and removed a gun from a half-opened drawer.

"Try the other drawer," Hamilton said. Ramon did so and came up with a second gun.

"Can't really blame you," Hamilton said. "Thieves and robbers everywhere these days. Well. Embarrassing silences bother me. Let me reintroduce you to each other. Behind the desk, Major-General Wolfgang Von Manteuffel of the S.S., variously known as Brown or Jones. Beside me, Colonel Heinrich Spaatz, also unimaginatively known as Smith, Mr. Joshua Smith, also late of the S.S., Inspector General and Assistant Inspector General of the north and central Polish concentration and extermination camps. Thieves on a colossal scale, murderers of old men in holy orders, and despoilers of monasteries. Remember, that's where you last met—in that Grecian monastery where you cremated the monks. But, then, your bunch were specialists in cremation, weren't you?"

The stillness in the room was total. All eyes were on Hamilton with the exception of those of Von Manteuffel and Spaatz: They could see only each other.

"Sad," Hamilton said. "Very sad. Poor manners. Spaatz came all this long way to see you, Von Manteuffel. Admittedly, he came to kill you, but he did come. Something, I believe, to do with a rainy night in the Wilhelmshaven docks?"

The sharp crack of a small-bore automatic tore through the silence. Hamilton looked at Tracy,

who, gun loose in an already nerveless hand, was
sinking to the floor. From the state of his head, it
was clear that he would never rise again. Maria had
a gun in her hand; she was pale.

Hamilton said, "My gun is on you."

She put her automatic back in her bush jacket
pocket. "He was going to kill you."

"He was," Ramon said.

Hamilton looked at her in bafflement. "*He* was
going to kill *me*, so *you* killed *him*?"

"I was waiting for it."

"I do believe," Navarro said thoughtfully, "the
young lady is not all that we thought she was."

"So it would seem." He said to her, "Whose side
are you on?"

"Yours."

Spaatz at last looked away from Von Manteuffel.
He stared at her in total incredulity. She said quietly,
"It is sometimes difficult to tell one Jewish girl from
another—or sometimes even from other women."

Hamilton said, "Israeli?"

"Yes."

"Intelligence?"

"Yes."

"Ah. Would you like to shoot Spaatz too?"

"No."

"No? Some form of prejudice?"

"They want him back in Tel Aviv."

"Failing that?"

"Yes."

"My apologies, and without any reservations.
You *are* becoming unpopular, Spaatz. But not yet

in Von Manteuffel's class. The Israelis want him, too, for obvious reasons. But the Greeks"—he nodded to Ramon and Navarro in turn—"those two gentlemen are Greek army intelligence officers —want you for equally understandable reasons." He looked at Hiller. "They supplied me with those gold coins, by the way." He turned back to Von Manteuffel. "The Brazilian Government wants you for dispossessing the Muscia tribe and for killing many of them. And *I* want you for the murder of Dr. Hannibal Huston and his daughter, Lucy."

Von Manteuffel smiled and spoke for the first time. "I'm afraid you all want a great deal." He sat back in his chair. "And I'm afraid you're not going to get it."

A loud crashing of glass caused most of them to turn and simultaneously the barrels of three sub-machine guns protruded through three smashed windows.

Von Manteuffel rose and barked, "Any person found with a gun on him will be shot on the spot. Do I have to tell you what to do next?"

He didn't. All guns were dropped to the floor, including two that Hamilton had not known that Spaatz and Hiller were carrying.

"So." Von Manteuffel nodded in satisfaction. "So much better than a blood bath, don't you think? Simpletons! How do you think I have survived for so long. By taking endless precautions. Not just guns in drawers, Mr. Hamilton. But items such as the little press button my right foot rested on."

He broke off as four armed men entered and

atched them in silence as they searched the cap-
ves for other weapons. They found none.

"And the rucksacks," Von Manteuffel said.

Again the search failed to turn up a weapon.

Von Manteuffel said, "I would have a word with
ıy old friend Heinrich, who appears to have come
very long way for nothing. Ah, and this man."
Ie indicated Hiller. "I gather he's an accomplice of
ıy dear ex-comrade in arms. The rest—take them
nd their pestilential luggage across to the old grain
tore. I shall be subjecting them to some intensive
nd, I fear, painful questioning." He put a hand on
Maria's back and pushed her violently toward the
loor. She fell onto the broken glass and began to
leed.

"On the other hand, perhaps not. I shall decide
bout the questioning after I've had my chat with
Ieinrich."

ELEVEN

THE OLD GRAIN STORE WAS BUILT entirely of beautifully cut and fitted stone; stones fitted without mortar. It was twenty feet by twelve, and had three storage bins on either side. The sides and the partitions of the bins were made of heavy adze-cut wood. A single weak and naked electric lamp, suspended from the ceiling, burned in the center of the store. There were no windows and only one door opening. But without a door. The presence outside of a man with a cocked machine carbine would have made a door superfluous anyway. There were no furnishings of any description. Hamilton and his fellow captives had nothing to do but look at each other or at the sentry, who faced them, his elderly but no doubt still lethal Schmeisser leveled directly at them: He had about him the desperate, bored look of a man who was yearning for an excuse to use it.

Navarro finally broke the silence. "Well, I fear

for the health of our Mr. Smith—or Spaatz, as w
say now. Hiller, too, for that matter."

"Never mind about *their* damned health," Han
ilton said. "Start thinking about your own. Whe
he's finished with those two, who do you think
next on his list? Whether or not he indulges in
little torture, a little intelligence gathering befor
hand?" He sighed, and touched a handkerchief t
Maria's skin where the glass had cut her. "Tru
old trusty secret agent Hamilton to tell all. Vo
Manteuffel knows who I am, who Maria is, an
who you two Greek so-called intelligence office
are. He can't let us live and he can't let Silver c
Serrano live either—obviously."

"Speaking of Serrano," Serrano said, "could
have a word with you?"

"Go ahead."

"In private, if you please."

"If that's what you want, come into my office.
The two men moved to a corner of the room wher
Serrano spoke in a low rapid tone. Hamilton lifte
his eyebrows and his face registered surprise, a
emotion he practically never betrayed. Then h
shrugged his shoulders, nodded twice, turne
thoughtfully, and looked at the sentry. He rejoine
the group.

"Big man," Hamilton said quietly to Ramor
"My size. Black from head to toe—beret, jacke
trousers, shoes. I want those clothes. More impo
tantly, I want that gun. Even more important,
want them both fast."

"Easy," Ramon said. "Just ask him."

Hamilton didn't reply. They watched him. Turning away so that his back and Ramon's were to the guard, he savagely, and to the accompaniment of the indrawn hiss of Maria's breath, bit the ball of his left thumb. At once the blood began to flow. He squeezed the torn flesh until the blood flowed even more freely, then smeared it over Ramon's uncomprehending face.

"All in the interest of art," Hamilton told him. "Brother, what a fight this is going to be."

The "fight" started as they moved to a corner of the store, just out of the sentry's line of sight. The sentry would have been less than human not to want to see the source of the sound of the heavy blows which began, and the shouting and swearing. He moved forward into the doorway.

Hamilton and Ramon were belaboring each other mightily, fighting in vicious fury, kicking and punching, intent on inflicting grievous bodily harm. The sentry was curious, confused, but not suspicious. He had a heavily brutal face behind which there was no great threat of intelligence.

"Stop that!" he shouted in German. "You madmen! Stop it or—"

He broke off as one of the combatants received a murderous blow and came staggering to fall flat on his back, half in and half out of the doorway, eyes turned up in his head, the face masked with blood. The sentry stepped by him, ready to quell any further signs of trouble. Ramon's hands closed round his ankles. Navarro's closed around his arms. And Long John Silver swung a fist at his throat.

Four men prepared to carry three blanket-covered, stretchered forms from Von Manteuffel's room. Von Manteuffel said, "It can be fatal to allow an enemy to live longer than is necessary." One of his men looked up, *"Where?"* He paused, briefly, for thought. "Over the side with them. Think of all those poor starving piranha. As for our other friends in the grain store, I don't think now they can supply me with any more useful information. You know what to do."

"Yes, Herr General," one of the men said. "We know what to do." His face was wolfish in anticipation.

Von Manteuffel glanced at his watch. "I expect you back in exactly five minutes. Don't delay. Come back after you've given the piranha their second course."

The guarding figure, dressed in black, faced the grain store with a leveled Schmeisser in his hands. He heard the sound of footsteps some way off and glanced quickly over his shoulder. Four men—the four who had disposed of Spaatz and Hiller—were about thirty yards away: Their machine carbines were shoulder-slung. The dark figure looked back at the open doorway of the grain store. He waited until his ears told him that the approaching group were no more than five yards away, then swung round with his Schmeisser blazing.

In the ringing silence that followed, Maria said n a subdued tone, "You play for keeps, don't you? Did you *have* to kill them?" She looked at her hands. "I guess we all play for keeps."

"I didn't want them to kill us or have one second to think about it. I looked like their buddy until they got close. You don't play footsy with cornered rats. Those are desperate men and you can bet that each one is a trained, efficient, and practiced killer. I don't much feel like apologizing."

"And no need," said Ramon, who, like his brother, had remained unmoved by the proceedings. "The good Nazi is the one who has stopped breathing. So. Five guns. What do we do?"

"We stay here because here we're safe. For now. Von Manteuffel may have thirty, forty men—maybe more. Out in the open we'd be massacred."

He glanced down at the stirring figure of the sentry. "Ah! Junior is coming to. I think we'll send him for a little walk so that he can apprise his boss that there's been a slight change in the status quo. Should give Von Manteuffel quite a turn."

Von Manteuffel was making notes at his desk when the knock came on the door. He glanced at his watch and smiled in satisfaction. Exactly five minutes. Just over two minutes since he had heard the burst of machine-gun fire. He called out permission to enter, made a final note, said, "You are very punctual," and looked up. His expression of surprise vanished and his eyes opened almost impossibly wide. The stumbling, stunned, bruised,

bleeding figure before him was clad only in hi
underclothes.

The store was deep in shadow. The single lamp
had been switched off. What little light there wa
came from a newly risen moon.

"Fifteen minutes and nothing," Navarro said. "I
that good?"

"It's inevitable," Hamilton said. "We're in dark
ness. Von Manteuffel's men are exposed, or woulc
be if they showed themselves, and they don't dare
show themselves. What can they do? Smoke us ou
if the wind is right? But no wind, so no smoke."

Ramon said, "Starve us out?"

"We should live that long."

The time crawled by. Apart from Navarro, who
stood by the doorway, everyone was lying down
They may have been trying to sleep for some hac
their eyes shut but were unquestionably wide awake
Navarro said, "Two hours. That's two hours gone
now. Still nothing."

"Would you mind, watchman? I'm trying to
sleep."

Hamilton sat up. "Don't think I will sleep. They
are up to something. I've no cigarettes. Anybody?
No?"

Serrano proffered a packet.

"I thought you were asleep. Thanks. You know
Serrano, I wasn't quite sure whether or not to believe what you told me. But I believe you now i
for no other reason than the fact that it has to be

as you say. So I guess I owe you an apology." He paused, "God. I've got to stop this. Apologizing seems to have become a habit."

Ramon said curiously, "May we know what the present apology is about?"

"Of course. Serrano is government. On the need-to-know principle, I suppose, Colonel Diaz kind of forgot to tell me."

"Government?"

"Ministry of Culture. Fine Arts."

"God help us all," Ramon said. "I would have thought there were enough genuine vultures in those godforsaken parts without adding . . . what you call culture vultures to the list. What on earth are you doing here, Serrano?"

"That's what I hope to find out."

"Splendid. Such candor. Señor Hamilton?"

"I told you, I only learned about him a couple of hours ago."

Ramon looked at him reproachfully. "Señor Hamilton, you're at it again."

"At what?"

"Being enigmatic. Evasive."

Hamilton shrugged and said nothing.

Serrano said, "An honest doubt doesn't require an apology."

"There's a little more to it than that," Hamilton said. "I thought you were Hiller's man. Back in Romono, that is, when I first met you. I'm afraid I'm the person who clobbered you. I'll give you back the money I took from your wallet. Not much I can do about your stiff neck. Forgive me."

"Forgive, forgive," Maria said. "I don't suppose anyone is going to forgive me."

There was a brief silence, then Hamilton said, mildly enough, "I have apologized."

"Apologies and forgiveness are not the same thing. You're clearly of the opinion that my association—that's the nicest way I can put it—with the Nazi bastard who called himself Smith was unforgivable. It all depends upon who is doing the judging, who is casting the first stones. All four of my grandparents died in Auschwitz. The chances are high that it was Von Manteuffel or Spaatz who sent them there. Or both. I suppose the world is tired of hearing about it, but six million Jews died. Was I so wrong? I knew if I stayed with Spaatz long enough he'd lead me to Von Manteuffel, and we really wanted him, too. I knew of only one way of staying with him. So I—we—found Von Manteuffel. Was I so wrong?"

"Tel Aviv?" Hamilton made no attempt to conceal his distaste. "Another of those barbaric Eichmann show trials?"

"Yes. But not a show. A trial and punishment. And a lesson for the future."

"Von Manteuffel will never leave the Lost City."

"This Dr. Huston," Serrano said carefully. "He meant so much? And his daughter?"

"Yes."

"You were here at the time they—ah—died?"

"Murdered. No. I was in Vienna. But a friend of mine—Jim Clinton—was here. He buried them. He even gave them a tombstone and inscription—

burned on wood with a red-hot poker. Von Manteuffel killed him also—sometime later."

"Vienna?" Maria said. "Wiesenthal? You're with the Institute?"

Serrano said, "What's this, young lady?"

"You should watch those slips of the tongue, Mr. Serrano, calling me a lady. The Institute is a Jewish central organization for hunting down war criminals. Based in Austria, not Israel. Mr. Hamilton, why can they never let the left hand know what the right is doing?"

"Same old need-to-know principle, I suppose. All I really know is that I had a double reason for hunting Von Manteuffel down. Got close to him twice in the Argentine, twice in Chile, once in Bolivia, twice in Kolonie 555. An elusive character, always on the run, always surrounded by his thugs. But I've caught up with him."

"Or the other way around," Serrano said.

Hamilton remained silent.

"Your friends are buried here?"

"Yes."

"I'm hungry and I'm thirsty," Navarro said plaintively. It was half an hour before dawn.

"I am deeply moved by your sufferings," Hamilton said. "What's a damned sight more important is that you're alive. I didn't want to depress anyone any more than they already were by saying what was on my mind, but I didn't think we'd see the night out."

Ramon said, "How could they have gotten to us?"

"Simple. Lots of ways. With a small cannon, a rocket launcher, any kind of antiaircraft gun, or a mortar. They could have directed two or three very nasty pounds of high explosive straight through this open doorway. Maybe the shrapnel would not have got us all, but the concussion in this confined space would have finished us off. Or they could have crawled over the grain store roof from the back and lobbed in a few grenades or a stick or so of blasting powder. The effect would have been the same. Maybe they didn't have any of those materials on hand, which I don't believe for a minute— Von Manteuffel lugs around with him enough weaponry and artillery for an armored battalion. Maybe the idea just didn't occur to them, which I don't believe either."

"So why didn't they?"

"I think that Von Manteuffel believes, as he has reason to, that we are dangerous in the dark. That we might be deployed outside. He's waiting for daylight before moving in for the kill."

Serrano said unhappily, "It will be daylight soon."

"Yep, it will, won't it?"

In the first faint glimmering of light Maria, Serrano, and Silver stared at Hamilton without comprehension as he extracted the camera from his haversack, opened it, released the flap to display the transceiver, extended an aerial, and spoke into the microphone.

"Night Watch," Hamilton said. "Night Watch." The speaker crackled and the reply was immed-te.

"We have you, Night Watch."

"Now."

"Now it is. How many vultures?"

"Thirty. Forty. A guess."

"Repeat after me, Stay under cover. Napalm."

"Stay under cover. Napalm." Hamilton switched f. "Useful, no? Very thoughtful is Colonel Diaz."

"Napalm!" Ramon said.

"You heard the man."

"But napalm. How about us?"

"Very tough, those airborne commandos. But, ɔ, they won't use it directly. They've no intention f dropping the stuff on us. They'll ring the area. ot a new technique but intimidating."

Hamilton made another switch on the camera nd a faint bleeping sound could be heard.

"Homing signal," Ramon explained to no one in articular. He looked at Maria. "How else do you ink they'd ever locate this place?"

"I didn't ask. I'm really smart, for a girl. You've ɔt everything organized, haven't you?" Maria ɔunded slightly bitter. "Never thought to tell us?"

"Why should I? Who was telling anybody any-ing true?" Hamilton said.

"How long will they take to get here?"

"Twenty minutes."

"And dawn is in about the same time?"

"About."

"It's getting light already. They could attack be
fore your friends get here."

"Unlikely. In the first place, it'll take Von Man
teuffel and his minions some time to get organized
and if we can't hold them off for a few minute
after that then we've no right to be here in the firs
place. Second, as soon as they hear the sound o
the helicopter engines they're going to forget al
about us."

It was becoming lighter, but still the courtyar
remained deserted. If Von Manteuffel and his me
were preparing to launch an attack, they were bein
discreet about it.

By and by Silver said, "Engines. I can hear ther
now. Coming in from the south."

"I don't hear them myself, but if you say they'r
coming in, then they're coming in. Do you see wha
I see, Ramon?"

"Yes, indeed. I see a man on the roof of thei
mess hall with a pair of binoculars to his eyes. H
must have good hearing, too. The legs?"

"If you would."

In his typical one-sweep movement Ramon lifte
his rifle, froze, and squeezed the trigger. The ma
with the binoculars collapsed to the roof. Afte
some seconds, he scuttled crab-wise away on tw
hands and a knee, dragging a useless leg behin
him.

Hamilton said, "Our friend, General Von Man
teuffel, must be losing his cool or he wouldn't hav
taken a stupid liberty like that. I don't think we'
be seeing any more sky watchers." He paused.

The sound of the plane engines was now unmis-
akable and increased rapidly in strength as the
raft approached: Finally, the rackety clamor of the
ngines reached an almost intolerable pitch as three
arge gunships began to descend between the re-
erberating walls of the cliffsides.

Hamilton said, "Inside."

Maria paused in the doorway. "Okay to look?"

Hamilton pushed her roughly inside and behind
wooden partition where he joined her.

"Napalm, you ninny. Some of that stuff could fly
oose."

"What about rockets? Bombs?"

"Jesus. For a smart dame, you're a dummy. This
a historic monument."

Moments later, almost having to shout to make
erself heard over the clamor, she said, "That awful
mell."

"That's napalm. And the smell's not the worst of
"

"Shouldn't we—shouldn't we go out and help
hem?"

"Help them? We'd only be in their way. Believe
he, those lads don't require help of any kind. And
as it occurred to you that they'd probably mow
s down before we got three paces beyond that
oorway? They don't know who we are. Airborne
ommandos have the odd habit of shooting first
nd asking afterward who you were. A little discre-
on and patience, please . . ."

The calm came within two minutes. The sound
the helicopter engines died away. A klaxon

sounded, presumably to indicate an all clear. No
one shot had been fired.

Hamilton said, "I think the intrepid Captai
Hamilton and his gallant crew may now safely ris
a peek outside." They filed out through the ope
doorway.

Three gunships stood in the courtyard before th
ziggurat. The ruins of the ancient city were ringe
with smoke from the still burning napalm. At lea:
fifty commandos, tough and competent and arme
to the teeth, had their guns trained on about thre
dozen of Von Manteuffel's followers, while fou
commandos, one carrying a carton of handcuf
which had been brought along for the purpos
moved along them securing their wrists behin
their backs. In the forefront of the captives was Vo
Manteuffel himself, already handcuffed.

As Hamilton and the others reached the center c
the courtyard an officer advanced to meet them.

"Mr. Hamilton?" he said. "Major Ramirez. A
your service."

"Thanks. You've already been of more tha
enough service." They shook hands. "We are mo:
grateful. That really was efficient."

"My men are disappointed," Ramirez said. "W
had expected a rather more—ah—challengir
training exercise. You wish to leave now?"

"Within the hour, if we may." Hamilton pointe
to Von Manteuffel. "I'd like to speak to that man

Van Manteuffel was brought forward betwee
two soldiers. His face was gray and without expre
sion.

Hamilton said, "Major Ramirez, this is Major-General Wolfgang Von Manteuffel of the S.S."

"The last of the infamous Nazi wartime criminals, no? I do not have to shake hands?"

"No." Hamilton looked unwaveringly at Von Manteuffel. "You have, of course, murdered Colonel Spaatz. And Hiller. Along, of course, with Dr. Huston, his daughter, scores of Muscias, and God knows how many others. To every road there is an end. With your permission, Major, there are a couple of things I would like to show Von Manteuffel."

First, he asked that certain tools be gathered. Then, accompanied by soldiers armed with shovels, powerful electric torches, and two large battery-powered floodlights, the group made its way toward the base of the ziggurat.

"This ziggurat is unique," Hamilton said. "Every other known one is solid throughout. This one has been hollowed out and honey-combed like the great Egyptian pyramids. Please follow me."

He led them along a winding, crumbling passage-way until they came to a low, vaulted cavern, smooth-walled, with no further passageway. The floor was covered with broken fragments of rock and gravel to a depth of between one and two feet. Hamilton spoke to Ramirez and indicated a sector of the floor. Eight soldiers with shovels immediately began to excavate this area. In a short time an area six feet by six had been cleared to reveal a square slab of stone with an inset iron ring at either end. Crowbars were inserted into the rings, and the slab, not without considerable difficulty, was lifted clear.

A shallow flight of stairs led down from the open-ing in the cavern floor. They moved down these, along a rough-hewn passage, and halted before a heavy wooden door.

Hamilton said, "Well, Serrano, this is where you come into your own. As for you, Von Manteuffel, let your last reflections be the most ironic you've ever had. You'd have given your heart and your soul—if you ever had one—for what lies beyond that door. But you sat atop it all those years and never knew it was there."

He paused, as if deep in thought, then said, "It's a mite dark in there. There are no windows or lights. If you would be so kind, Major, have your men switch on all torches and floodlights. I'm afraid the air will also be a bit musty, but it won't kill you. Ramon, Navarro, give me a hand."

The door proved to be reluctant to yield, but with a sepulchral creaking sound, it eventually did. Hamilton took one of the floodlights and passed through, the others crowding close behind.

The large square cavern inside was hewn from the solid rock. All four sides had stepped rock shelves cut into them to a depth of fifteen inches. On them was a spectacle that was beyond belief: The entire cavern gleamed and glittered with thou-sands upon thousands of artifacts in solid gold.

There were bowls, crocks, crockery. There were helmets, shields, plaques, necklets, busts, and fig-urines. There were bells, flutes, ocarinas, rope chains, vases, breastplates, openwork headdresses, filigree masks, and knives. All in gold. There were monkeys, alligators, snakes, eagles and condors, pelicans and vultures, and innumerable jaguars, all in solid gold. And for good measure there were seven open boxes, sparkling and glittering with precious stones, more than half of them emeralds. It was a treasure-house exceeding the dreams of avarice.

It seemed as if the stones spoke, as if the other silence would last forever. Serrano, at last, was the first to speak.

"The lost treasure of the Indies. The El Dorado of a million dreams." He knelt, picked up an emerald. The flash of color was a magnification of light. "The Spanish always believed that some vanished tribe had taken with them a huge treasure trove. Mankind has believed in the myth ever since, and thousands have lost their lives in the search for the El Dorado. But," he said, shaking his head, "it was no myth, no myth."

It was clear that Serrano was scarcely capable of believing the evidence of his eyes.

"It was a myth, all right," Hamilton said. "But the golden treasure was there, all right. It was just that everybody looked for it in the wrong place—up in the Guianas. And they all looked for the wrong thing—they thought it was royal Inca gold. It wasn't. The people who made those were the Quimbaya of the Cauca Valley, the greatest masters of the goldsmith's art in history. For them gold had no commercial value, it was solely a thing of beauty."

"And the Spaniards," said Serrano, "would have

melted the lot and sent it back to Spain in ingot form. Mr. Hamilton, you have done my country, and you have done the world of art an immeasurable service. And you were the only non-Indian alive who knew of this. You could have been the richest man alive."

Hamilton shrugged. "Once a Quimbaya, always a Quimbaya."

Ramirez said, "What will become of this?"

"It is to be a national museum," Serrano said. "The rightful owners, the Muscias, will return and become the custodians. Few people, I'm afraid, will ever see this—just accredited scholars from all over the world, and but a few of those at a time. The Brazilian Government—who don't even know the location of this place yet—is determined that the Muscias, what's left of them, will not be destroyed by civilization."

Hamilton looked at Von Manteuffel, who was gazing, trancelike, at the fortune that had lain beneath his feet. He was stunned.

Hamilton said, "Von Manteuffel."

The general turned his head slowly and looked at him like a sightless man.

"Come. One last thing to show you."

Hamilton led the way into another, much smaller cavern. Side by side at the far end lay two stone sarcophagi. Above each was a plain pine board with poker-burned inscriptions.

Hamilton said, "A friend of mine did those, Von Manteuffel. Jim Clinton. Remember Jim Clinton? He came looking, too. You should. After all, you

nurdered him shortly afterward. Read them. Read
hem aloud."

Still in the same odd, sightless fashion Von Man-
euffel looked slowly around, looked at Hamilton,
and read tonelessly:

"Dr. Hannibal Huston. R.I.P."

"And the other?" Hamilton said.

*"Lucy Huston Hamilton. Beloved wife of John
Hamilton. R.I.P."*

Everyone stared at Hamilton. Shocked comprehension came slowly, but it came. Von Manteuffel's
eyes flickered once in recognition. Then he said, "I
am a dead man."

Hamilton, with Maria close to his side, and with
Ramon and Navarro, Von Manteuffel, and the
others trudging closely behind, made their way to
a helicopter at the edge of the courtyard only yards
from the rim of the plateau. Suddenly Von Manteuffel, wrists still handcuffed behind his back,
broke away from the commandos and started to
run. He was heading for the edge of the cliff.

Ramon started after him, but Hamilton caught
him by the arm. Ramon looked startled.

"Let him be," John Hamilton said. "You heard
him. Let him be right, for once in his life. He's a
dead man."

ABOUT THE AUTHOR

Alistair MacLean was born in Scotland. During World War II he served with the Royal Navy and was a school teacher until 1955. That was the year his first novel, H.M.S. ULYSSES, was published. That novel put him in the ranks of internationally best-selling authors, and he has remained there ever since with over twenty novels including THE GUNS OF NAVARONE, WHERE EAGLES DARE, SEAWITCH, GOODBYE CALIFORNIA, and ATHACASCA. In addition to his widely acclaimed status as an author, he is a screenwriter.